THANKFUL

By Shelley Shepard Gray

Sisters of the Heart series
HIDDEN
WANTED
FORGIVEN
GRACE

Seasons of Sugarcreek series
WINTER'S AWAKENING
SPRING'S RENEWAL
AUTUMN'S PROMISE
CHRISTMAS IN SUGARCREEK

Families of Honor
THE CAREGIVER
THE PROTECTOR
THE SURVIVOR
A CHRISTMAS FOR KATIE (NOVELLA)

The Secrets of Crittenden County
MISSING
THE SEARCH
FOUND
PEACE

The Days of Redemption series
DAYBREAK
RAY OF LIGHT
EVENTIDE

Return to Sugarcreek series
HOPEFUL

THANKFUL

Return to Sugarcreek Series, Book Two

SHELLEY SHEPARD GRAY

AVON
INSPIRE

An Imprint of HarperCollinsPublishers

"Peanut Butter Pie" recipe from *Simply Delicious Amish Cooking* by Sherry Gore (Zondervan, 2012) reprinted with permission.

This book is a work of fiction. The characters, incidents, and dialogue are drawn from the author's imagination and are not to be construed as real. Any resemblance to actual events or persons, living or dead, is entirely coincidental.

HarperCollins books may be purchased for educational, business, or sales promotional use. For information please e-mail the Special Markets Department at SPsales@harpercollins.com.

FIRST EDITION

Library of Congress Cataloging-in-Publication Data

Gray, Shelley Shepard.
  Thankful / Shelley Shepard Gray.
    pages cm.— (Return to Sugarcreek ; book two)
  ISBN 978-0-06-220447-9 (pbk.)
    1. Man–woman relationships—Fiction. 2. Amish—Fiction. I. Title.
PS3607.R3966T53 2014
813'.6—dc23
                                     2013048647

14 15 16 17 18   OV/RRD 10 9 8 7 6 5 4 3 2 1

To my agent, Mary Sue Seymour, who years ago
mailed me an article about a group of Mennonites in
Pennsylvania adopting children born to incarcerated
parents—and sparked a whole series.
Yes, miracles do happen to those who believe!

Call on me when you are in trouble, and I will
rescue you and you will give me glory.

Psalm 50:15

If you can't have the best of everything, make the
best of everything you have.

Amish Proverb

prologue

Ten Years Ago

"Betcha can't put your skates on as fast as I can!" Christina shouted as she ran down the hill toward the frozen skating pond.

Aden Reese grinned as he watched his neighbor plop on the ground, hike up her blue skirts to her knees, yank off her boots without untying them, and then at last stuff each foot into a snug white leather skate. Christina was two years younger than him—twelve years to his fourteen. Most boys he knew wouldn't be caught dead playing with a twelve-year-old.

But Christina?

Well, there was something about her that he'd never been able to ignore. It wasn't just her golden hair and light blue, almost silver eyes. No, it had more to do with her easy smiles. And the happiness that radiated from her.

It was also the way she never acted sorry for him when she realized that his parents were so busy with their handcrafted furniture business that they often left him alone for days at a time.

And the way she'd merely stood by his side two weeks ago, saying nothing when he learned that their van had gotten into an accident and they'd both died instantly. Instead, she'd slipped her slim hand into his and hadn't even flinched when he'd clung to it like a lifeline.

Christina was special to him. She was his friend. And one day? Well, she wouldn't be too young, and neither would he. Then he would court her properly until she agreed to marry him.

Until then, he would simply bide his time and look out for her.

"Aden, how come you're walking so slow?" she called out. "I'm ready to skate. What's wrong?"

"Me? Oh, nothing. Just a little cold, I guess. Um, will you be warm enough?"

She practically rolled her eyes. "*Jah*. I have on mittens, a cloak, a wool scarf, and even a bonnet over my *kapp*. You don't even have your coat on."

"I don't need it like you need yours."

"I'm not a child, Aden."

"I know that." Unfortunately, he knew that too well. Without wasting any more time, he sat down next to her and carefully removed his skate guards, then deftly switched out his boots for the skates. "Ready?"

"I've been ready. You know how anxious I am to try out my new skates!" She gingerly walked down the path toward the pond's edge, grasping his hand for support when he stepped to her side. She gave him a little smile of thanks before pushing off and gliding across the ice. With a feeling of satisfaction, he followed.

Time seemed to stand still as he skated by her side, her voice ringing in the chilly air as she told him the latest stories about her brothers and sisters. He smiled, happy to hear her chatter, just content to be doing anything other than thinking about how he was now all alone.

After they'd skated along the perimeter of the pond twice, she teased him again. "Betcha can't catch me now, Aden!" she cried as she sped forward, racing across the middle of the pond looking beautiful and ethereal.

Right until the moment he heard a sharp *crack* and watched her fall through the ice.

His heart froze. "Christina?" he called out, skating around the edge until he got to where she was.

Her head popped up. She gasped. Her skin was already blue, her eyes panicked. Before he even considered the best plan of action, he jumped in.

The water was jarringly cold, though the temperature barely registered. All he felt was her body as he cupped his hands under her arms and pushed her upward. *Please, God, please, God, please, God,* he repeated to himself as they broke the surface.

And the Lord must have heard him, because He gave Aden the strength to push Christina out of the water and onto the ice. Then the Lord gave Aden the strength to pull himself out, using an overhanging branch for support. A branch that he hadn't noticed before.

Seconds later, they were on the bank and he was throwing his blessedly dry coat over her body and breathing life into her mouth.

Wonder of wonders, she finally gasped, inhaled, coughed, and then brought up what had to be a quart of pond water. And her eyes opened. "A—"

"Don't talk." He pressed his lips to her forehead. "Shh," he added as he yanked off both their skates, shrugged her into his coat, picked her up, and ran to her house. The whole time praying like he never had before.

"Please, please, please," he murmured over and over again

as he ran barefoot through the frozen fields, across the front yard, and up the front walkway to her house. Her parents must have seen him coming because they were already running to meet him, taking her from his arms and rushing her upstairs to a hot bath.

The moment she was out of sight, he knelt on their spotless kitchen floor and prayed. He prayed until his voice was hoarse and his throat was sore. Until Mrs. Kempf came downstairs and announced that Christina was going to be just fine, but that he needed to change out of his wet clothes right quick or he was going to get sick.

Her warnings hardly mattered to him, however.

His prayers had already been answered.

chapter one

January third was, without a doubt, his least favorite day of the year.

For the last ten years, Aden Reese braced himself before he walked downstairs. Sometimes, he had to stop halfway down, take a few deep breaths, and remind himself that the family meant well. Then he would finally school his features into a twisted combination of pleasure and surprise when he approached the family gathered around the table.

This year, unfortunately, was no different.

"Aden, at last you are here!" Martha Kempf exclaimed as she rushed to his side and promptly threw her arms around him. "We were beginning to wonder if you were ever going to come downstairs."

After the slightest hesitation, he hugged his adoptive mother back and forced himself to smile. "I'm sorry, I guess I'm a lazybones today."

Martha patted his cheek. "Today is your day, Aden. You can be anything you want," she added as she pulled out his chair. "Now, sit."

As he sat, he smiled at the family surrounding him. Joe, his adoptive father, looked right back, his eyes moist. Just as they always did on this day.

Beside Joe, twelve-year-old Leanna looked at him in that bashful way she always did. Treva gazed with her usual somber expression. The boys, Nate and Henry, eyed him with a combination of respect and awe.

And Christina? Only Christina looked a bit amused. As if she were the only one who had the slightest inkling that he hated being the reason for so much fuss.

In the middle of the table lay all his favorites—sausage and bacon, scrambled eggs and waffles. A pecan coffee cake. Orange slush and canned peaches. It went without saying that Martha and the girls had been up for hours preparing the feast.

The lump that was lodged in his throat now threatened to choke him.

Because they were all waiting, he said the same thing he always did every January third. "*Danke* for this fine meal. But, truly, there was no need to go to such fuss."

"Of course there is," Martha said. "Today marks the day you saved Christina's life. We will always, always be thankful for your bravery, Aden."

Joe nodded. "Always. Now, let's give our thanks and eat."

Aden closed his eyes and tried to simply concentrate on giving his thanks to God. And thanking the hands who had created the bounty. But all he could think about was how thankful he was that everyone had stopped staring at him.

Next, serving dishes were passed around, each one to him first. Each time, he took his portion, and then passed the serving dishes along to Christina. More than once, their fingertips brushed against each other. More than once, she blushed before quickly looking away.

Little by little, conversation began. Joe talked with Nate and Henry about jobs he wanted them to do at the farm. Martha cautioned Leanna not to be late for school.

Christina asked Treva about her new job at the fabric store in the Alpine Village shops.

At last the meal was over. After thanking everyone again, Aden was more than ready to escape the house and drive his buggy to the livery in Sugarcreek. From there, he would take a van to his new job at the hospital.

"Aden, I know you're short on time, but could ya still take Christina into work?"

"Of course."

Christina met his gaze for the briefest of seconds before speaking. "I'll be ready in five minutes, Aden. All I have to do is put my lunch together. And yours, too, of course."

He felt his cheeks heat. He hated all these traditions! "I can make my own lunch, Christina."

"I don't mind. I promise, it's almost ready."

"Take your time, then. I'm in no great hurry."

"We made you a special lunch today," Treva told him with a wide grin. She had her father's dark brown eyes, and they looked as full of mischief as always. "We even put in three brownies."

He bowed slightly. "I will enjoy them *verra* much." And though the chocolate-caramel concoctions would likely taste like sandpaper in his mouth, he knew he'd never tell them differently.

But he did need a breather. Gazing over Treva's head, he said, "Christina, just come out whenever you are ready. I'm going to go hitch the buggy."

Two minutes later, with his wool coat thrown over his shoulder, he escaped to the barn.

When he was completely alone, his footsteps slowed and he forced himself to remember the day of her skating accident. It was truly one of the worst days of his life.

He still acutely remembered his panic. The fear that had overcome him for days and had interrupted his sleep for months—he'd been so afraid he would lose her forever. But overriding it all was his extreme sense of guilt. A better friend would have looked out for her more closely. Would've inspected the ice before letting her race away.

A better man would have admitted that he should never be praised for that day. A better man would have never accepted a room in their loving household.

Unfortunately, he'd always found it easier to keep silent instead of refuting their belief in him. And he definitely never allowed them to guess his deepest, darkest secret. After ten years living as her sibling, he still was in love with Christina Kempf.

There Aden was, standing beside the buggy, lost in thought and looking as handsome as ever. Since he still hadn't noticed her, Christina took a moment to stare and let herself have a little moment to hope and dream. To imagine that he was her beau. To pretend that he was waiting for her because he couldn't stay away.

Instead of waiting for her because her mother had asked him to.

Then, as he blinked and focused on her, she rushed forward, taking care to keep her voice easy and breezy. Carefree. "I'm so sorry. It took me a little longer than I expected to get my things together."

"There's no reason to apologize. See, I'm only now hitching up the buggy."

"My, you really are moving slowly today," she teased. "Perhaps Mamm is right. Maybe we do need to make January third your own special holiday."

His mouth tightened. "If we could take this day off the calendar forever, I'd be grateful."

She knew how he felt. Though no one suspected, she still dreamed about the accident at least once a week. It was always the same nightmare. She'd relive the incident, hearing again the crack of the ice under her feet, feel the painful rush of icy water on her skin, followed by the burst of panic when she couldn't breathe.

Then she would jerk awake in a cold sweat. Her heart would be pounding and she'd be gasping for air.

And then it would take at least another hour for her to calm down enough to drift back into sleep.

What her parents seemed to forget was that the skating accident was all her fault. She'd had a terrible crush on Aden when she was twelve and was constantly doing everything she could to try to impress him. That day, it had included skating as fast as she could across the pond. If she had been looking at the ice instead of imagining him gazing at her in admiration, she would have realized that the ice had begun to crack.

If she'd been smarter, she would have saved them both a lot of trouble and he never would have almost died from a terrible case of pneumonia.

Looking back on those days, she ached to rewrite history. Without a doubt, she had embarrassed them both multiple times a week with her puppy love. After all, who would ever take a young girl's infatuation seriously?

"Maisey's hitched. Are you ready to go?"

"But of course." Without waiting for his help, she climbed into the buggy and scooted right next to him, positioning her tote bag as she did.

When the skirts of her light green wool dress brushed against his leg, he stiffened before scooting another inch or two to his left. "So, what are your plans for the day?" he asked as he jiggled the reins and encouraged Maisey to begin her trot down the driveway.

"The usual things, I suppose. I'll work in the kitchen at the inn."

His lips thinned. "Are those ladies letting you do more than wash dishes yet?"

"Sometimes," she said as he directed his horse to turn left and they began the fifteen-minute journey to her job at the Sugarcreek Inn.

"It's not right, the way they have you standing at the sink from the time you get there until the moment you leave."

"I'm the youngest and the newest employee. You know how it goes, Aden. Besides, Marla let me help her make rolls the other day."

"Do you want me to talk to them? You know, remind them that you were hired to cook and serve, not just be a dishwasher?"

"Definitely not!"

"You sure? I don't mind."

"Positive. Besides, Mrs. Kent said that she's going to hire a new girl to wash dishes now that Miriam's left. I think that was her way of telling me that I'm getting a promotion of sorts."

"*Gut.*"

As they got closer to the Sugarcreek Inn, the traffic around them got a bit heavier. Christina kept silent, knowing Aden needed to keep his attention on the vehicles trying to pass them. Maisey was a calm horse, to be sure. But that didn't mean she didn't have moments of skittishness.

At long last Aden pulled into the Sugarcreek Inn's parking

lot. After guiding Maisey to one of the hitching posts at the back of the lot, he hopped out.

Christina knew by now that he would take it as a personal offense if she merely climbed down from the buggy and went on her way. For some reason known only to him, Aden always liked to help her down.

"What time do you get off today?" he asked when he appeared at her side.

"Four o'clock."

"Do you need a ride?"

"I'm not sure. Probably Mrs. Kent or Ruth can take me home. I'll ask them," she answered as she slipped her right hand in his while his right curved around her waist. For the briefest of moments, they were as close as they'd ever been. Just long enough for Christina to smell the soap on his skin and look into his caramel-colored eyes.

Then all too soon she was standing firmly on the ground and Aden was stepping away.

"I'll call the restaurant around two o'clock to make sure you have a ride," he said.

She didn't dare tease him about this. He took her safety very seriously. "All right. I'll know who will be taking me home by then."

"*Gut.*"

He had just turned around, and when she knew she couldn't let another moment go by without saying something, she added, "Aden, even though you don't like celebrating today, I'm grateful for it. I will always be grateful for you jumping in the pond and pulling me out. For saving my life."

A myriad of expressions crossed his features—pain, remembered fear, embarrassment. She knew each one by heart because she'd felt the same things.

But then he took her hand in his, curved both of his around it, and pressed. "It was a life worth saving. I, too, will always be thankful for that day, Christy. Always."

Then with his cheeks a brilliant red, he turned around as she slowly walked into the restaurant.

She had a new tingle on her skin. After ten years, she'd never given up on the thought that Aden might someday be hers. Every time she was sure that there was no chance of them having a future, something like this would happen, making her heart soar all over again.

But of course, she knew better than to do anything to encourage him. The last thing in the world she wanted was to embarrass them both.

She'd done enough of that for two lifetimes.

chapter two

"Watch yourself today, Christina," Marla whispered into her ear as Christina neatly placed her coat and lunch container on her hook at the back of the restaurant. "Jana is in a terrible mood this morning."

"Again?"

"Again." Marla shrugged her shoulders, the movement in obvious sympathy. "I can't figure it out. Business seems good, the customers seem happy enough."

"Maybe it doesn't have anything to do with the inn, then."

"If it doesn't have anything to do with the restaurant, what could be wrong? All Jana does is work." After peeking around the corner, she added, "I don't know what's going on, but I wish she'd take out her bad mood on other folks besides us. I'm getting right tired of it."

Christina mentally agreed, but didn't dare risk saying anything out loud. She was lucky to have this job and she certainly didn't want to risk it by talking badly about the restaurant's owner. "More dishes today?"

Ruth, the kitchen's other worker—and the only one of the three of them who wasn't Amish—trotted over and gave her a little hug. "Aren't you just the sweetest thing?" she said with a smile. "I was just telling Jana that you'd probably wash dishes all day, every day for the next year if we let you. But I've got some super news to share."

"And that is?"

Ruth pointed to a young girl. "This is Jolene. She's our new dishwasher."

Christina smiled warmly and extended her hand. She didn't want the young girl to realize how thrilled she was with this news.

"Hi, Jolene," she said politely. "I'm *verra* glad you're here."

As Jolene shyly smiled, Ruth grinned in a far bolder way. "I had a feeling you would be excited to see our new girl. Now, off you go."

"To do what?"

"You're going to be a server this morning."

"Truly?" She didn't even try to hide her excitement.

Marla came over and stood next to Ruth. "*Ach*, but your eyes are so wide, Christina! You look like it's Christmas and your birthday, all rolled into one."

"I'm just *verra* thankful that I won't be washing dishes all day long. Not that there was anything wrong with it, of course," she said to Jolene.

"I don't mind it," the new girl replied.

Reaching around Christina, Ruth pulled out a crisp white server's apron and pressed it into Christina's hands. "Slip this on and go on out to Jana. She's going to supervise you herself this morning. And good luck with that."

Unable to help herself, Christina traded glances with Marla.

Marla shrugged. "She's in a mood, but she likes you, dear. Don't worry, she'll be patient."

After tying on her apron, Christina walked toward the swinging door that separated the kitchen from the dining area. "It's times like this that I really miss Miriam," she murmured.

"I know. Miriam would have teased ya, and then would

have probably been your shadow all day, watching over you like a doting mother hen," Marla agreed. "But she's a house-wife now. And a mighty happy one at that."

Christina smiled. After working at the Sugarcreek Inn for more than five years and pretty much being the backbone of the restaurant, Miriam and Junior Beiler had gotten hitched in a whirlwind wedding. It had been a big one, and somewhat of a grand occasion since they'd decided to hold the recep-tion right there at the inn. Even the bishop had approved such a move, taking into consideration that the two of them had known each other so long that there was no need to wait to wed.

But the short engagement had meant that there was no time to reserve a kitchen wagon. Christina, Marla, Ruth, Jana, and about a dozen more girls had worked in the restau-rant's kitchen, making chicken, stuffing, and even an assort-ment of wedding cupcakes for the happy couple.

Practically the whole town had attended, and it had been quite the loud and boisterous celebration.

But now all of that was over. Long over.

"Hurry now, Christina," Ruth called out. "If you don't get a move on, Jana's going to hustle in here to see what's keep-ing you."

That was all the encouragement she needed. With a deep breath, she walked through the doors and felt her cheeks heat when some of the customers looked at her curiously.

Mrs. Kent smiled at her as she approached. "Ready for today?"

"*Jah*. I'm eager to be a waitress."

Mrs. Kent chuckled. "I'm glad you feel that way. I know you're going to do great. I'll stay by your side for a few tables, then you can be on your own."

"So quickly?"

"Don't worry, Christina. It's just food. If you mess up the order, it can always be fixed. And all you have to do if you do run into trouble is ask me to join you."

After giving her a pad of paper and a pencil, Jana went through a few points, then had Christina shadow her the next hour. By the end of the hour, Christina was feeling comfortable enough to do all the talking. At that point Jana seemed content to stand by her side and listen.

As the restaurant began to fill with the lunch crowd Jana gave her a little push toward the back tables. "It's time we split up, dear. Just do things like you did them with me and you'll be just fine."

And wouldn't you know it? She was fine. Since she'd worked in the kitchen she was familiar with all of the dishes and was therefore able to answer most questions. Next thing she knew, she was taking a break, then darting back and forth from the tables, taking orders, delivering glasses of tea and lemonade, and refilling coffee cups.

She was doing so well, she was caught off guard when Jana called her over to take a phone call. "Aden is on the line," she explained. "He wants to know if you need a ride home. Do you?"

"Oh, I was so excited about waitressing, I forgot to ask if you could take me home today. Can you? Ruth has other plans." Jana usually never minded taking a few minutes to get out of the restaurant.

"I'm sorry, but I can't do it today. I've got a meeting with my accountant at five."

Spirits sinking, she took the receiver from Jana. "Hi, Aden."

"Hi. How are things in the kitchen?"

"For your information, I'm not working in the kitchen."

"Oh? What are you doing?"

She couldn't help the excitement from seeping into her voice. "I just happen to be waitressing today."

He chuckled. "Is that a fact? Well, good for you. I can't wait to hear all about it."

Little by little, her excitement faded. He was sounding very much like a doting uncle, which was nice, but it wasn't quite the response she'd hoped for. "I will tell you everything. When we have time to talk, that is."

He chuckled. "I'm sure that will be sooner rather than later. So, do you need me to pick you up today?"

"I'm afraid I do."

"You do?" She heard a couple of papers being shuffled and something clanging in the background. "All right, then," he said around a sigh. "I better go tell Janice that I'm going to have to leave soon."

"Who is Janice?"

"She's one of my supervisors. Look, I might be a few minutes late, but don't worry. I'll be there as soon as I can."

Now she felt even more like a child. "I'm sorry for the trouble."

"It's no trouble, Christy. I told you, no matter what, I'll always look out for you. Always and forever."

Yes, he had told her such things. And she'd always counted on his promises. But, unfortunately, today she was feeling like yet another responsibility for him. Feeling even more deflated, she said, "All right. Um, see you around four."

Hanging up the phone, she wondered if anything would ever change between them. If today's conversation was any indication, it was obvious that all her hopes and dreams were destined to remain merely figments of her imagination.

"He certainly seems like a caring person," Jana murmured

from behind her shoulder. "I couldn't help but overhear. He's going to drop everything and come get you?"

"*Jah*. Well, he's going to tell his supervisor that he needs to leave to come get me."

"Well, that's what brothers do for their little sisters."

Something about that bothered her to no end. She was tired of making him into something that he wasn't. "Aden is very caring and kind. But he is definitely not my *bruder*."

A pair of fine lines appeared between Jana's brows. "I'm sorry. I thought he lived with you?"

"Aden does, but he's not my *bruder*. He's only lived with us for ten years."

Jana rested her hands on her hips. "Hmm. Well, all right, then. Now, you'd best go take care of table twelve. I think they're ready to give you their order."

Christina pulled out the little notepad from her apron and got to work, only a little embarrassed that she'd been so curt with her boss. But there were some things she just couldn't joke about.

And her mixed-up relationship with Aden Reese was one of them.

Over at the cash register, Jana Kent scanned the last hour's receipts with a sinking heart. It seemed that no matter what she did, she wasn't achieving the increased bump in business she'd been so hoping for.

She'd never imagined that her life would be so stressful at fifty-eight. Of course, she hadn't imagined Harrison would have died suddenly twelve years ago. At forty-six, she'd become a widow and sole proprietor of an Amish restaurant that had been her husband's dream, not hers.

At first, she'd welcomed the business and the work. She'd been proud of herself for being independent, glad to be so busy, and so grateful for her employees. Most of the women were Amish and had taught her quite a bit about patience and faith. They'd become good friends, too.

But now she was wishing she were one of the women she was currently serving meals to. She'd like nothing more than to hop in her car and go for a long drive.

The fact was, she was tired. She spent too much time worrying about bills and money and schedules and employees, and not enough time on the pain in her joints, the smiles on her grandchildren's faces, and the comfort of her couch at home.

Her goals had become about taxes and profits, not about taking trips or starting hobbies.

Something needed to change, but she just wasn't sure what to do. How did one go about changing a life?

Her four children would say that she'd brought this on herself. Harrison had left her enough money to take care of her needs for the rest of her life. It had been her stubbornness and a desire to honor her husband's memory that had kept the restaurant going.

Only now did she realize that while she'd been honoring Harrison's memory, years and years had passed. Her children had married and had children of their own. Far too many times she'd put off visits to them because of her many commitments at the restaurant.

A playful wave in front of her nose brought her back to reality. "Jana, you planning to give me my change anytime soon?"

With a start, Jana realized she'd been clutching her friend Pippa Reyes's ten-dollar bill like it was a lifeline. "I'm sorry, Pippa. It's been a long day."

Pippa gazed at her in concern. "That's not good, my friend. It's barely three o'clock."

Jana tried to laugh it off. "Yes. It really is not good."

Pippa reached out and patted her hand. "Why don't you come over to my house tonight? I'll make you some tamales and we'll talk. I'll be more than happy to help you in any way I can."

Pippa Reyes was a new transplant to Sugarcreek. Her brother worked at the brickyard and had often commented to her over the years about how much he enjoyed the wholesome, quiet and quaint atmosphere of the Midwestern town.

Pippa, still recovering from a painful divorce, had seized upon her brother's invitation to join him and his wife in Sugarcreek.

In short order, she'd found an apartment in the middle of town, gotten a part-time job at the Walmart in Millersburg, and had settled into life in rural Ohio.

She and Jana had started talking one afternoon over a slice of pie and had soon discovered that they had many things in common. Now they got together once or twice a week and caught up on the latest news. Jana considered Pippa to be her best friend.

Though Jana knew spending some time with her girlfriend would be wonderful, she simply didn't know how she was going to be able to fit in one more thing with her schedule. "I'd love to come over, but tonight's not good."

"Make time. I'm worried about you," Pippa said, her voice lilting the way it did whenever she grew concerned about something. "I think you need a friend right now." After a second she added her trump card. "Besides, in addition to making tamales, I've got cheese enchiladas and pintos in the fridge. Manny came over with his boys yesterday, and I have leftovers."

There were some things Jana just wasn't strong enough to resist. And tamales and cheese enchiladas were one. They sounded wonderful; so completely different from the kind of food they served at the inn. She smiled at her friend. "Is eight o'clock too late? I've got a meeting with the accountant at five o'clock and I don't know how long it will take."

The dimple in Pippa's cheek appeared. "It's not too late at all. I'll have a plate waiting for you."

"Bless you, Pippa."

Her girlfriend playfully shook her finger at her. "Just don't forget. You need some time to rest and relax. I'm sure of it, *chica*."

Looking around the restaurant, Jana smiled wanly. For the record, she was sure about that, too. She needed to make a change very soon. Very, very soon.

chapter three

It was taking every ounce of strength Judith Knox had not to reach out and clasp her husband's hands. But of course she couldn't do it. Showing such emotion wasn't something that was done, and she wanted to be sure she was acting completely properly.

Not that the social worker would know all that much about proper etiquette for Amish wives. No, Miss Bernadette Fogle didn't seem to be the type of woman to put much stock in things like that. In the three times they'd met, Miss Fogle—Bernie to pretty much everyone she knew—had been much more concerned about their love for a baby than if they were everything proper.

And thank goodness for Bernie's easygoing demeanor, too! Over the last few months, Judith had had some challenging moments. After suffering a miscarriage and hearing the news that she couldn't ever give birth to a baby of her own, it had taken her weeks to lift herself up from a deep depression.

Only through the grace of God, the patience of her family, and Ben's love had she begun to accept the possibility of adoption.

It had been a difficult process. But now that they were in the middle of it, Judith felt only anticipation and excitement for what was to come.

As if she'd noticed Judith's jiggling knee, Bernie smiled

softly. "Judith, there is nothing to be nervous about. Remember, your paperwork and interviews went very well. You two have been deemed to be exceptional candidates for adoption."

As Judith exhaled in relief, her husband leaned forward, resting his elbows on his knees. "Bernie, do you have news for us today? I fear Judith and I are on pins and needles here."

After a pause, Bernie smiled. "Actually, I do have news. I've come to ask if you would consider being foster parents for a time. You know, while you're waiting to adopt."

Ben frowned. "I'm afraid I don't understand."

Bernie crossed her legs, visibly searching for the right words. "Well, on occasion, we have a need for a family to take in a newborn. For a time."

"For a time?" Judith echoed, finally finding her voice.

Bernie nodded. "It's, ah . . . a special situation."

"We'd appreciate it if you spoke a bit more directly," Ben said, his voice hinting at his growing impatience. "This is hard enough on my *frau* without you talking in circles."

Judith's heart went out to him. Not caring anymore about how it would look, she scooted closer to him. If she couldn't hold his hand, she wanted to feel his support at the very least.

"Tell us about this baby, Bernie."

"It's a little boy. His name is James." Bernie's expression softened before she continued. "There's no easy way to say this. His mother is in the correctional facility in Marysville."

It took a moment to understand what Bernie meant. "His mother is in prison?"

"I'm afraid so." She leaned back against the couch. "About ten or twelve years ago, some Mennonite and Amish families in Pennsylvania were asked to help foster some prisoners' children. It was a successful partnership. The families cared for the babies and young children like they were their own, giving them lots of love and support—the things that are the hallmarks of your community. Recently, we've decided to try out this program in our county and state."

Judith felt her throat tighten as disappointment sank in. "So you are not asking us to adopt this baby? Just keep him for a bit?"

"Yes. Until his mother can care for him, or his family has presented themselves as capable alternatives."

Ben frowned. "But this is not what we asked for, Bernie." His voice hardened. "We filled out the paperwork to adopt a baby. Not to watch over some . . . some prisoner's child."

Bernie studied him before quietly putting the papers she had resting on her lap back in her leather tote bag. "You are exactly right. This wasn't what you asked for. But it's my job to find a home for this baby. Surely you can understand my point of view? My priority is to always put the children first," she added as she stood up. "I couldn't resist coming out here and giving it a try."

"I can't fault you," Ben said quietly. "I also feel sorry for the babe. But I have to admit to not being too happy with you at the moment, Bernie. We thought you had news for us. Poor Judith here had her hopes up. Please don't—"

"I'm okay, Ben," Judith said quickly. "Bernie is exactly right. A baby's needs are far more important than my wishes at the moment." Turning to Bernie, she smiled. "And you're right. I can't fault you for trying."

Bernie's eyes warmed. "Thank you for understanding, Judith. When I have some news about available babies, I'll be sure to let you know."

It all sounded so final. "It's going to be a long wait, isn't it?"

"Yes. It's as I told you from the beginning—adopting a

child isn't for sissies," she said with a slight smile. "It's a long process. It could be weeks or months—but it will most likely be at least a year. But don't despair. I feel certain that sooner or later your day will come."

As those words sank in, Bernie picked up her tote from the couch and slipped it onto her shoulder. She already had her keys in one hand, and her cell phone in the other. It was obvious that the social worker wasn't going to rest until she had a home for baby James.

Suddenly, Judith knew what she had to do. "Wait!" she called out.

Bernie paused. "Yes?"

"Um, I know James needs a home right away, but could you let us have until tomorrow morning to talk about this?"

A true look of sympathy entered Bernie's expression. "It's only to foster him, Judith. I can't promise that he'll ever be up for adoption. . . ."

"I know. But he needs a home, *jah?*" Giving in to temptation, Judith reached out and gripped Ben's hand. "We need a baby to care for. I mean, I need a baby. Can we call you tomorrow? Please?"

"Well—"

"In the morning?" Judith asked quickly. "Ben and I . . . We could call you at seven. That's not too early, right? I'll go right down to the phone shanty and give you a call."

Ben whispered in her ear. "Are you sure about this, dear?"

Judith nodded. Suddenly, she knew she'd never been more sure about anything in her whole life.

Bernie bit her bottom lip as she looked from Ben to Judith. "Are you sure you even need a conversation? I'm not trying to hurt your feelings, but if you're not serious—"

Ben squeezed Judith's hand, answering a hundred questions

without Judith needing to say a single word. "We are serious," he said. "Please, give us until seven tomorrow morning."

The line that had been between Bernie's brows slowly eased. "All right. Until seven. You have my cell phone number, right?"

"It's written down in about five different places," Ben joked. "Believe me, we have it."

"Until tomorrow morning then," Bernie said as she turned the door handle and headed out the door.

Only when the social worker's car disappeared down the road did Ben speak again. "Judith, what are you thinking?"

"That I need this baby, Ben."

A myriad of expressions appeared on his face. After staring at her hard, he pointed to the couch. "In that case, I think we'd better sit back down. It seems we have a lot to talk about and little time to do it."

At four o'clock that afternoon, Christina sat down with a sigh at one of the two-person tables in front of the picture windows that lined the front of the Sugarcreek Inn. As the muscles in her body eased, she kicked out her legs and stretched her arms lightly in a most unladylike way.

She didn't care though. She felt a terrific sense of satisfaction about all that she'd accomplished.

Goodness, but she'd worked so hard! Learning to be a server was tougher than it looked. In addition, running back and forth from the kitchen with meals and pie and coffee and . . . well, *everything* took more than a bit of coordination and planning! Never had she been so thankful to have black tennis shoes on her feet.

Through it all she kept thinking about Aden and how impressed he would surely be when he heard about how well she'd done. Just imagining how pleased he was going to be made the generous slice of lemon chess pie she was eating taste even better.

Mrs. Kent had given her the slice of pie when her shift was over. "You did a good job today, Christina," she'd said. "Every time I looked, you were on your feet, bustling to the kitchen or visiting with customers. You've earned yourself a break and a snack. Take a moment and enjoy a treat," she said before she'd left for the bank.

Though usually Christina would have felt self-conscious about eating a slice of pie when all of her friends were still working, she accepted her boss's offer with a grateful smile. Her feet hurt, her nerves were frayed, and, unfortunately, she had been unable to stop thinking about Aden, and the difference between what he'd said and what she'd wished she'd heard.

As the minutes ticked by, moving from four o'clock to a quarter after and then four thirty, much of the elation she'd felt slowly ebbed away.

She stood up to get a cup of tea and then sat back down to watch the clock some more. As the minutes passed, she picked at the remaining half of pie, which suddenly didn't taste all that good anymore.

And began to worry. Aden was late. Really late. It was now almost five o'clock.

After taking her plate to the kitchen, she tried to put things into perspective. Aden was likely stuck in traffic or maybe he'd had a difficult time getting out of work early. No doubt he was probably wishing that he was doing anything else besides running to pick her up from her job.

Then the door blew open, bringing the one person who

had always interested her just a little too much. "Aden!" she called out happily before rethinking her greeting. Here, again, she was acting a bit childish when she should have been showing him that she was a grown woman.

But whether he thought her childish or not, he turned right toward her. His lips curved in what had to be a mirror image of hers—a true combination of happiness and relief. "I'm sorry I'm so late. I had a time of it, getting out of the hospital when I was supposed to. Were you worried I'd forgotten?"

"I knew you hadn't forgotten."

Pulling his black stocking cap off his head, he shook his golden-brown hair away from his eyes. "Boy, it has gotten cold out there. I doubt the temperature has made it past the teens today."

She got to her feet. "I'll bring you a cup of *kaffi*."

"Danke." As he watched her walk across the almost-empty restaurant, he said, "I hope you weren't too worried. Sometimes I feel like I'd give a pretty penny for the use of a cell phone for five minutes."

She smiled. She'd certainly thought that a time or two. After placing a mug of steaming brew in front of him, flavored just the way he liked it, with only a small dash of cream, she finally replied, "I was fine."

Taking a sip of coffee, he stretched out his legs. "This tastes great. They had me transporting patients all day today. I barely had time to eat."

Although it was obvious he was trying to hide it, he kept glancing over to a young couple eating steaming bowls of vegetable soup two tables over.

"Aden, are you hungry? Would you like a piece of pie? Or maybe even a bowl of soup?"

"I would, if it's not too much trouble. I didn't get much of a chance to eat today."

"Not even your special lunch we packed you?"

"I'm afraid that was gone by eleven this morning."

"Even Treva's brownies?" she teased.

"Especially Treva's brownies. Everyone at the hospital loves them."

"I'll go get you whatever you would like. Remember, today is your day." Of course, the instant she said that, she regretted her words. She knew how much he hated to be reminded of that day. He'd even told her again that morning.

She scanned his face. Sure enough, there was a thread of irritation in his eyes.

And just like that, a new tension had appeared between them. "I'm sorry I brought it up."

"Don't worry about it." His hands curved around his mug. "I shouldn't be so sensitive, we both know that. So . . . is there any coconut cream pie to be had?"

"There's always that, Aden," she teased. "I'll be right back."

When she got to the kitchen, she said hello to some of the girls who worked the supper shift and went ahead and sliced Aden a generous portion of pie herself. As she walked to him, she knew that no piece of pie could make amends for her thoughtless comment.

"Aden, I don't know why I brought up it being your day. Especially since we'd both decided not to mention it."

"It's nothing. I've got thick skin by now." He forked a good-sized portion and popped it into his mouth. "Good pie."

"I'll let Marla know." She edged into her seat and watched him eat. And then before she knew it, she blurted out what was on her mind. "Aden, do you ever think of me in a special way?"

He stilled. "In a special way?"

"You know . . . " She shrugged. "Like I'm something more to you than the girl you saved ten years ago."

He choked, and his fork landed on the table with a clatter. After she patted his back and offered him some ice water, he glared at her. "Why in the world are you asking me something like that?"

"No reason," she said quickly. Because, really, how could she even begin to explain all of the things she'd been thinking about him? "I mean, no reason beyond the fact that today is the anniversary of your rescuing me."

"There must be some reason."

"I don't know. I guess it's because someone called you my brother today."

He looked as shocked as she'd felt. "I'm definitely not your brother."

She smiled, glad that she'd brought up the topic for discussion. "I agree." Feeling a little bit braver, she said, "As a matter of fact, I've never thought of you like a brother." If only they were alone! Then maybe, just maybe, she would have the nerve to share how she really felt about him!

Eyeing her, he leaned back in his chair. "I've never thought of you as a sister. Hmm . . . I suppose I'm more like your guardian."

"My . . . my guardian?"

"*Jah*." His smile turned complacent. "I think that's a real *gut* fit, don't you?"

"Not especially." Unable—actually unwilling—to keep the hurt out of her voice, she said, "Why in the world would you think of yourself as my guardian?"

"Well, you're the eldest. And you have no brothers to look after you."

"I have Nate and Henry."

"You know what I mean. They're fourteen and fifteen." Relaxing again, he picked up his fork and jabbed another chunk of pie. "And while your parents are the nicest folks I've ever met, they've got their hands full with the house and the farm and the animals and such. So I've always thought I had better take on that role."

She wasn't enjoying the picture he was painting of her: someone to be looked after. As a duty. A chore. "Aden, I have done my share of looking after my sisters and brothers. I have a job and a lot of responsibilities, too. I don't need a guardian. And I certainly don't need you to feel obligated to look after me."

Back down went that fork. "Christina, why are you so peeved?"

"Because you're seeing things all wrong."

"Truly? How would you describe me? How do you see our relationship?"

Frustrating. That's how she would describe their relationship.

And as for him? Well, she would describe Aden Reese as tall and lean with hair the color of dark honey and matching eyes. Competent and calm. Steady and sturdy. And handsome, of course. To her, he'd always been so handsome. . . .

Buying herself some time, she teased, "I think you know what you look like, Aden."

"Come on, tell me what you think of me." His eyes had turned more serious. And the way he was looking at her hinted that he was as apprehensive about what she was going to say as she'd felt about his words.

And so she prevaricated. "I think of you as a friend."

For a split second, something flared in his eyes that looked a whole lot like disappointment, but it was quickly hidden. "*Jah*, I would say we had a real good *friendship*."

"There's nothing like being *friends*." Sure, it wasn't what she really wanted. But it was better than considering him her sibling.

Finally, he took another bite of pie. Then another one. "You know, there's nothing at all wrong with thinking of each other as good friends. Obviously, that's what we are, right?"

"Right."

"I mean, why else would I be the one to take you places?"

"Why else?" she said brightly.

But inside, she felt like a part of her heart had just shriveled up and died. For some reason, Aden seemed intent on making sure she knew exactly how he thought of her. And how he wanted their relationship to stay.

Today might have been his special day, but it was perfectly obvious that it needed to be a special day for her, too.

She needed to stop confusing gratitude with love. Stop confusing infatuation with romance.

She needed to stop loving Aden Reese. She needed to stop that, right this minute.

The road back to the Kempf house had never felt so long. As Maisey meandered down the long, dirt and gravel private lane that led to their sprawling house, Aden knew that something needed to change—and fast.

He couldn't continue with the way things were with Christina any longer. For too long he'd been pretending that things could always stay the same between them.

But it was mighty obvious now that they certainly never

could. The Lord gave each one of them a responsibility to be the best disciple of his character that was possible. That meant that each man and woman needed to become someone to be proud of.

And he was not proud of the way he thought about Christina. He'd been lying through his teeth when he'd spouted all that nonsense about being a guardian and a *gut* friend.

No. In his mind, she was his. He'd saved her life. He liked her independent streak and easy smiles and her kind heart. She was also beautiful. He'd never seen a prettier girl.

To make matters worse, he'd secretly loved her for years. Sometimes it took everything he had not to touch her. Hug her hello. Give in to temptation and brush his lips against her cheek.

And, yes, to maybe even do more than that.

And staying longer at the Kempfs' house, taking advantage of their warm hospitality and giving nature, was not the right thing.

He needed to move out soon. Before he did something that would shock Christina.

And then? Then he was going to need to begin looking around for another girl to court. Someone suitable. Someone whom he could grow to love and not feel conflicted about.

Someone who didn't think of him simply as a friend.

Someone who wasn't part of the best family he'd ever known.

chapter four

It was six in the morning, and Judith and Ben had already been up for two hours.

"Time has never moved so slowly," Judith grumbled as she sipped her coffee and watched the kitchen clock pass time like an obstinate donkey on a country trail.

Beside her, Ben grinned at her statement, though she noticed that he didn't refute her words. "The day does seem long already. I sure wish time passed this way when we're sleeping. I can never get enough sleep."

"Maybe we'll soon get even less," she teased.

"Maybe." His expression dimmed a bit. "Judith, do ya think we should go over to your folks' place and talk to them before we call Bernie back? Their advice might be worth listening to."

"*Nee.* I want this to be our decision, Ben. Yours and mine. Not my family's."

"You know your parents wouldn't try to force us to change our minds. They aren't that way."

"I know they wouldn't, but I don't want to have to explain myself. Or explain what fostering is all about." More to the point, she didn't want anyone to plant even the smallest seed of doubt into her dreams.

All night long she'd prayed about their decision and had asked the Lord to give her strength and patience, too. The longer she'd prayed, the more certain she felt that she was following His will.

Actually, she felt like she was meant to be a foster mother to baby James.

And even though it made no sense, she wanted to hug the feeling of anticipation to her chest as close as possible, for as long as possible. Soon enough their decision would be a topic of conversation around her family's kitchen table. For just a few more hours, she wanted things to be just between her and her husband. To enjoy this sense of peace and purpose.

Ben nodded, but still he gazed at her in a worried way. "Judith, dear, you do understand that fostering this baby ain't the same as adopting it, right? I mean, Bernie sounded certain that this would be a temporary thing."

"I understood. Of course, I understood that." Not even to Ben would she admit that in the middle of the night she'd also prayed to keep the baby.

"All right," he said slowly. "But . . . I know you, Judith. I fear that you're already imagining our life with this baby for years and years."

"I know the difference between fostering a *boppli* and adopting one, Ben."

Her husband leaned back as if stung, immediately making her feel ashamed.

"I'm sorry, I didn't mean to snap at you like that."

He sighed. "Judith, I'm not trying to be cruel. I just don't know if I can bear to see you get your hopes up, just to watch you become disappointed all over again."

"I won't." Though secretly, she did fear that that might happen. But she couldn't let her fears guide her decisions any longer. That was what she'd been doing for the last few months. In her heart, she knew she'd always be thankful for the chance to take care of a baby. Even if it was just for a little while. Because the idea of that baby had finally changed her perspective. It finally enabled her to begin living again. Yes, it might be very different from what she'd always imagined her life would look like. But it looked promising and full of joy all the same.

While she watched the second hand of the clock slowly eke its way around the numbers, Ben wiped down the spotless counters yet again.

After another two minutes, he threw down the dishcloth with a grunt of irritation. "I can't wait here another second. Let's walk down and leave Bernie a message."

She sprung to her feet. "Do you think that's allowed?"

"I don't see why not." He flashed a smile. "She said we'd most likely get her answering machine or voice mail anyway. Now when she checks her messages, she'll hear from us first thing this morning."

Feeling happier than she could remember feeling since she'd realized she was pregnant, she clasped her husband's hand and strolled down to the end of the street where the phone shanty was.

When they got to the small whitewashed structure, he squeezed her hand. "Would you like to leave the message, or shall I?"

She yearned to march into the shanty, dial the number, and tell Bernie that she and Ben wanted to hold little James as soon as possible. But she didn't trust her voice. She felt choked up, as if she was on the verge of tears. The last thing in the world she wanted was to start crying on the social worker's voice mail!

"I think you had better do it."

Instead of walking into the small enclosure, he paused and looked at her inquisitively. "Are you sure?"

She loved how patient he was with her. How he always seemed to know what she wanted, and even more important, what she *needed*. "I am sure." Before she could change her mind about anything, she handed him Bernie's business card.

Looking like he was preparing to jump off a cliff, Ben stepped inside and dialed.

The moment she heard the faint sound of Bernie's phone ringing, Judith leaned closer, eager to hear what he had to say.

"This is Benjamin Knox and we are leaving a message for— Oh! Oh, hello, Bernie." His eyes widened as he turned his head to catch Judith's eye. "*Jah*. We are up early. I guess you are, too."

He paused, looking at Judith once again. Obviously double-checking to make sure she hadn't changed her mind.

Judith nodded and made a motion with her hands for him to continue.

Repositioning the phone against his ear, Ben continued. "*Jah*, I mean, yes. We have made a decision. We would, indeed, like to be foster parents to James."

Eager to catch every bit of the conversation, she scooted inside the shanty, cramming herself to her husband's side.

Ben playfully nudged her with one of his elbows, pretending she was cramping his space.

But Judith was too excited to hear what was being said to play along. She leaned a little closer.

"Hold on one second, Bernie. Judith needs to talk with ya," Ben said with a smile. Then he handed the phone to Judith. "Talk to her. It's time."

She knew he was talking about far more than taking the phone call. It was time to cast away her regrets about not being able to conceive a child of her own. Time to put aside her disappointment about having to wait until God's timing was right to adopt a baby of her own. It was time to move forward and become a willing foster parent.

Maybe even past time.

Feeling as if she was finally moving forward, Judith took a deep breath. "Hi, Bernie. This is Judith."

"Judith!" Bernie said. "I can't tell you how happy I am to hear that you want to foster James. I visited with him yesterday afternoon. He is such a sweet baby."

And just like that, all of her doubts dissolved. Her heart melted. "I . . . I canna wait to meet him."

"Here's what happens next. I'll talk with the other people on James's case file. But if all goes well, I'll be bringing him out to your house tomorrow morning."

She felt her stomach drop. Glancing at her husband, she said, "Did you say tomorrow morning? That soon?"

Beside her, Ben tensed.

"That would be best," Bernie replied, her voice all business. "I need to pick up the paperwork from the office, and then go get little James from his temporary home. Plan on us arriving sometime between nine and ten." She paused. "Is that going to be a problem? We are anxious to get James with a caring family."

"*Nee!* I mean, it will not be a problem. We will be waiting for you." Somehow, some way, they would get everything together.

"Good. Very good." She paused. "I know you already have a crib. Do you feel like you will be able to get everything else you need for him by tomorrow morning?"

Judith felt like she was on a merry-go-round, her head was spinning so much. "As you know, my family owns a general store. And, um, my relatives have lots of baby things that I'm sure they will allow us to borrow."

"I was counting on you to say that." In the background, a phone rang. "Hold on for a sec." After a shuffle of the phone, and a couple of beeps, Bernie got back on. "Judith, I'm sorry, but I need to take a call. Do you need me to call you back? Do you have any questions?"

She was so stunned, she could hardly think straight! But through it all, there was only one thought that shined brightly. She was emotionally ready for this baby. "We don't have any questions. Bye, Bernie."

"Good-bye, Judith. James and I will be there tomorrow morning." And with that, their busy social worker clicked off.

Judith hung up her telephone far more slowly, then scooted around in the shanty to meet Ben's eye. "Bernie is going to bring James here between nine and ten tomorrow morning. We need to gather all the items we'll be needin' between now and then."

His gaze warmed. "Your voice is so breathless, you sound like you just ran a long race."

That was the perfect descriptor. In many ways, she had just run the longest race of her life. She'd tried for years to have a baby, then miscarried. Now she was about to foster a little boy who needed someone, who needed two people to love him. She had a feeling that they needed him just as much.

She was certain the Lord had guided them to this very point after a terribly hard journey.

"I feel like we just finished a race," she declared as they started their walk home. "Ben, a baby is coming to live with us! This time tomorrow morning we'll be waiting for Bernie and James to arrive!"

He laughed. "The Lord truly does work in mysterious ways. Very mysterious ways. Before you know it, you'll be holding him, Judith."

She felt as if she were the luckiest woman in the world. Truly blessed.

Then she realized two very important things. She had no idea about what to actually do with a baby. And they had an overwhelming number of things to do before James arrived. "Ben, we have too much to do! There's no way I'm going to be able to finish everything that needs to be done in time."

"You, my lovely wife, are exactly right."

"What?" She turned to him in surprise.

He curved an arm around her and gently squeezed. "There isn't any way you're going to get everything done in time. We need help. It's time to talk to your parents and your siblings, Judith. It's time to let them be here for us . . . just like we've been there for them over the years."

"How quickly can you hitch up the buggy so we can go to my parents' *haus* and break the news?"

"Ten minutes?"

"I'll be ready," she said with a smile.

For once, everything was going as planned. Everything was going to be just perfect.

Aden, you surely got up early. Were you aiming to beat the roosters today?" Joe teased when he met Aden outside by the barn.

"Nah, I've just got a lot to do."

"Never thought I'd see the day when a boy of mine was so eager to do chores."

Being referred to as his "boy" was almost Aden's undoing. He genuinely liked being a part of the Kempf family, and especially liked being so close to Joe and Martha. They were truly the parents of his heart.

But he forced himself to stay strong and ignore his weaknesses. Things had to change. They had to. He couldn't keep living with Christina. That was surely a recipe for disaster.

"I wasn't all that anxious to do chores, if you want to know the truth. It was more of a case of not being able to sleep."

"Oh?" Joe's expression turned concerned. "Something on your mind?"

"As a matter of fact, there is."

His adoptive father waved his hands, urging him to continue. "Well, don't lollygag. This waiting is making me feel like I'm on pins and needles. Spit it out."

"All right. It's like this. I, ah, have decided that it's time I moved out." He pulled off the black stocking cap that he favored in the winter and ran a hand through his hair, hating the stunned look of dismay that was steadily transforming his adoptive father's face.

"You sound awfully sure about this."

"I am." Aden looked away so he wouldn't have to watch Joe carefully arrange his features into a careful mask.

"I must admit that this is news to me. Matter of fact, I feel a little sideswiped. Have you been thinking about this for some time?"

"Awhile." *Twenty-four hours could count as awhile, right?*

"I see."

Aden rushed to explain. Well, rushed to try to come up

with an explanation that was close enough to the truth that Joe and Martha would believe. That maybe one day he could believe, too. "You know, I've been living here for a long time now."

"I know you have. A little more than ten years now."

"Ten years is a long time." He swallowed. Made himself say the words that he didn't quite mean. "A mighty long time, considering you all aren't my real family."

Just as if Aden had thrown a punch, Joe visibly flinched.

Aden couldn't fault Joe for reacting that way. He was hurting, too. This conversation was one he'd never wanted to have—the Kempfs had treated him far too well for him to ever minimize any of their kindnesses.

The only way he could justify this move was to think how his leaving was best for everyone. Especially Christina. Surely it would be better for Joe to assume Aden had grown restless and eager to be more independent rather than realize that the man the family had given so much to was repaying them by pining for their eldest daughter.

"I really do appreciate everything you and Martha have done for me," he added. "But I think I've overstayed my welcome."

Joe turned away, resting his hands on one of the rails of Maisey's stall and sighed. "Aden, I'm gonna be real honest with ya. I don't quite understand where all this is comin' from," he said after a lengthy silence. "Martha and I have always thought of you as part of our family. As far as I'm concerned, you're one of my boys."

"I realize that. You have always made me feel welcome. And of course I'm grateful for that."

Joe turned around and faced Aden. "To be perfectly honest, I've come to think of you as one of my own. Not that your parents shouldn't be remembered, of course."

"Of course."

"But if you haven't realized how special you are to us, I'm ashamed that we didn't do enough to ensure you knew that we felt that way. We love you, Aden."

The lump that had started to form in Aden's throat now threatened to choke him. He hated this. He hated making Joe feel like he had ever been less than an ideal father to him. But now, more than ever, he realized that leaving was the best thing.

He couldn't bear the shame of having Joe and Martha stare at him in disappointment if they ever suspected that his feelings for Christina were anything but sisterly.

Surely that would hurt far worse?

Treading carefully, he said, "Joe, you've been a *wonderful-gut* friend, and a wonderful father, too." After taking a fortifying breath, he added, "A better father than my own. You've done everything possible for me, more than I could have ever dreamed of."

Twin spots of color stained Joe's cheeks. "It was our honor."

"If it was, that says even more about what good people you and Martha and all the kids are. I can't think of another family who would have taken in an orphan like you did and given him so much for so long."

"You are a *gut* man, Aden. And you were a *gut* boy, too." He raised a hand when Aden threatened to interrupt him. "*Nee*, let me speak. I know you don't like to be reminded of saving Christina's life. I know you wish we wouldn't remember like we do."

"I will forever be grateful that I could help her. But, just so you know, there was no need for you to throw me a party every year. There was never any need for you to continually tell me thanks."

Joe smiled softly. "But see, that's the way of it, Aden. We want to always thank you."

"But—"

"Aden, we choose to remember. We want us all to remember how you jumped into that pond and pulled Christina out of the ice and water. Of how you breathed life into her lungs, and how you held her in your arms for a whole mile while you ran home barefoot. I don't ever want to forget the sight of you kneeling in our kitchen praying for her. It changed our lives." He swallowed hard. "It saved our lives."

He stared directly at Aden. Making him feel like he was a boy again. "From the time we met you, we knew you were a special boy," he murmured, his voice hoarse with barely suppressed emotion. "I don't want to talk badly about your parents, so I'll only say that they looked after you a bit differently than I would have wished. I felt like when the Lord gave us back Christina, he gave us you, too. You were our present. We've loved you for each day of these ten years."

Tears pricked Aden's eyes. And though it was unmanly to feel such emotion, he knew he couldn't hide how moved he was. "I feel very fortunate to have you and Martha in my life. I've loved being one of six *kinner*. All of you have given a lonely orphan quite a gift."

"But you are now ready to move on."

"I'm older now. Twenty-four. It's time I got a place of my own." Thinking quickly, he added, "Besides, I like my job at the hospital, and if I lived closer to town I could just walk to catch the van I take to work."

"That is true. Are you sure these are the only reasons, Aden? Are you positive that there's nothing else spurring you on?"

It felt as if Joe were staring through him. Reading more into his thoughts, reading his mind. Like he knew.

"I am sure. Please don't take this for anything other than what it is . . . a sign that I am growing up."

"Martha ain't going to like your news, you know."

Aden smiled softly. "That's why I told you first."

Joe seemed to weigh that for a moment. "Her feelings might not be too hurt if you tell her that you'd be willing to come over here to eat two nights a week."

"Two?"

"Sunday supper is a given. Surely one more night ain't too much to ask."

"Of course not. But—"

"*Gut,*" Joe interrupted, his voice firm. "We've been blessed to eat supper with you every evening, Aden. Don't make us give you up all at once."

"That is fair." He chuckled. Because they both knew that coming for supper two nights a week was going to be to his benefit.

Joe clapped him on the shoulder. "Let's feed and water the horses so we can get some breakfast. You know, if we don't hurry, Nate and Henry will eat us out of house and home."

"I'll do the water, you do the feed," Aden said.

"Don't make a mess, son," Joe cautioned.

Aden grinned at the familiar warning. It was the same thing Joe always told him. Just as him watering and Joe feeding the horses was the way they'd always divided the chores.

As he turned on the hose, Aden realized it was going to be yet another thing he was going to miss.

chapter five

Christina tried not to look like she was pouting. She truly did. But as they all sat together in the great room after supper and listened to Aden tell them his big news, she felt betrayed and dismayed.

And so very sad.

And if she was honest, more than a little angry.

For most of her life—well, at least the last ten years—she'd taken to leaning on Aden for just about everything. Since she was her parents' eldest child, she'd long felt the weight of responsibility of much of the chores on her shoulders. It had been nice to know that he, too, could handle some of her younger siblings' problems.

But even more than that, she had truly enjoyed being around him. She'd liked looking across the room and seeing him reading one of the hunting or fishing magazines he'd always liked so much. Even better, she'd enjoyed sharing amused glances with him when her parents said something particularly funny or when one of her brothers acted just a little too full of himself.

Now all that would be gone. Now *he* would be gone.

"I'm sorry, but I just don't understand," Mamm said for about the eighth time in as many minutes. "Aden, surely there isn't any hurry for you to be out in the world on your own." Her eyes widened. "Or is there a hurry? Are you unhappy?" Her eyes widened. *"Ach!* Has something happened?"

"Nothing's happened," he reassured her. "This isn't about me being happy or unhappy here. It's about moving forward."

Mamm looked skeptical. "Moving forward?"

"Martha, I'm talking about being older. About needing some space of my own."

"But . . . you have your own room." Her brow wrinkled. "Do you need a bigger room?"

"My room was fine. It *is* fine. But what I am trying to say is that I need more than that." Obviously agitated, he met Christina's eyes. Wrapped in his gaze was everything he was obviously feeling— frustration that his meaning was being misconstrued as well as humor in her mother's need to wrap everything up into something she could easily understand.

But overriding both those emotions was an unmistakable plea for help. And right then and there, Christina knew she had no choice but to back him up. Even though she didn't understand his decision, she couldn't refuse his need any more than she could refuse her youngest sister's need for hugs.

Clearing her throat, she said, "Mamm, Daed, you all are forgetting that Aden is not a child or a teenager in the middle of *rumspringa*. He's a grown man at twenty-four years of age! Why, many men his age are already married and have *kinner* of their own by now. How can we expect Aden to go courting when he's got a houseful of all of us watching his every move?"

Treva, ever the most level-headed of them all, nodded. "You know, that makes a lot of sense to me. I've certainly felt like I've been watched a bit overzealously from time to time."

"You needed watching, Treva," their mother declared. "Especially when you were seeing that awful Simon Beachy."

"Simon wasn't that bad."

"He wasn't that good," Daed said with a scowl.

"He kept trying to hold your hand," Leanna pointed out.

"And he was fat," Henry pointed out. "And had soft hands."

Obviously embarrassed, Treva tossed back her head. "See what I mean? I don't blame you one bit, Aden."

"*Danke*, Treva," Aden said with a dry smile.

Nate and Henry looked at each other and then sighed. "I understand, too, Aden," Henry said. "When I'm as old as you, I sure wouldn't want to be living at home and doing chores."

Their father grunted. "Because I'm sure when you're living on your own you'll have no chores to do."

"Not the same ones, though," Henry said.

Aden chuckled at all the bickering. "Oh, I'll have chores, I'm sure of that." Looking at Nate and Henry, he added, "I just won't have to do anyone else's too. Or have to take care to make sure everyone else is doing theirs correctly."

"I'll look forward to that day, too, son," Daed said with a dry expression. "Now, Aden, what do you need from us?"

"Nothing. Just your understanding."

Her parents looked at each other. "We understand, but that doesn't mean that we're happy about you leaving."

"Even if you live by yourself, I will still think of you as my eldest boy, Aden," her mother said. "No matter where you go, you always will be."

"I want to always be one of your boys, Martha. It would be my honor."

After that, there didn't seem to be anything more to say. Nate and Henry darted off, Treva hugged Aden before escaping to her room, and her parents patted his head before wandering into the kitchen.

All too quickly, only she and Aden remained. Christina felt so many conflicting emotions, she yearned to escape to her room so she could cry in peace. But when she noticed that he seemed just as stressed, she knew she couldn't leave him alone. "It looks as if it's just the two of us now."

His gaze warmed. "How do you think it went?"

"About as well as could be expected, I suppose," she said diplomatically. "You gave us a bit of a shock."

"All I'm doing is moving out."

"I know."

"I mean, it's not like we won't still see each other."

"That is true. But things will change. It's going to be different."

"It is time."

"Perhaps." She yearned to say more, to tell him how confused and conflicted she felt. But she decided to keep her thoughts to herself for a little bit longer.

"Christina, please don't be upset with me."

His tone was so sweet, so pleading, she found herself looking into his eyes yet again. "I'm not upset."

"You sure?"

"I know you'll be fine. I mean, everything changes, right?"

"I think so." He swallowed. "It's like the seasons, I suppose. We can't stop winter from coming or spring from arriving. Change is inevitable."

She knew that. And she agreed. But it didn't make what was happening any easier. She was disappointed that she wouldn't be sharing most of her meals with him. Sad that their relationship was going to change. Worried about their futures.

"I'll be fine living on my own, you know."

"I imagine you will." Though it hurt to say it, she knew

it was true. Aden Reese was the type of man who would be fine wherever he was. "Do you, ah, have enough money to rent an apartment?"

"I think so. I've been saving for a while."

Which meant that he'd been planning this move for some time. For some reason, that made everything seem worse.

Which, unfortunately, made her blurt her innermost thoughts before thinking better of it.

"Aden, why, exactly, do you want to be on your own? And I'm talking about the *real* reason. Not the one you just told us all."

"I just told you the real reason. Honestly, Christina. Don't make this into anything more than it is."

She hated when he adopted that smart, know-it-all tone! She was about to throw up her hands in frustration and leave the room when she took a better look at him. He'd looked bemused, but now there was the barest hint of wariness in his gaze.

She realized her instincts had been right. He was hiding something. "I still get the sense that there's another reason you are suddenly so eager to leave. A secret one."

He leaned back and his expression turned guarded. "You sound mighty sure of yourself."

"I am. What is it? Have you met someone while working at the hospital that you want to be courting?"

His eyebrows rose. "You think I've met someone?"

He looked so horrified, she felt embarrassed. But not enough to take her words back. "It's the only thing that makes sense. And as I said, you are the right age to be courting someone seriously. And as I said, a lot of men your age are married."

"That is true." He reached up and rubbed a knot out of his shoulder. "Um, actually, I have been interested in someone."

"You have?" Oh, but this conversation was getting worse and worse. It was a struggle to keep a calm, peaceful expression.

"Oh, *jah*." He glanced at her briefly, then looked away, suddenly interested in a small cut on one of his knuckles. "It's not serious or anything. But I definitely have had my eye on this lady."

Lady? "So, um, did you meet her at the hospital?"

"I did." He paused before looking at her directly in the eye. "I met her a few weeks ago, as a matter of fact."

"You never said anything."

"Christina, you know why I didn't. Your parents would have asked me a thousand questions. Plus, with her being English and all . . ."

She felt devastated. Completely devastated. "What is her name?"

"Name? Ah, why is that important?"

Because she wanted to know everything about the woman who was taking Aden from her! But of course she couldn't say that. Instead, she tried her best to act calm, cool, and collected. "Oh, no reason. I was just curious. I mean, I might have met her at the inn or something." A sick feeling settled in her stomach. Gosh, had he gone and fallen in love with someone she knew? She didn't know too many English girls, but she did know a couple.

She gulped. "Have I met her? Do I know her?"

"*Nee!* I mean, I'm fairly sure you wouldn't have."

"Aden, are you going to tell me her name?"

"I am definitely not."

"I promise I won't say anything to anyone."

"Which is all the more reason that you don't need to know anything more about my private life." Standing up, he treated her to a look that was definitely a little bit full of himself.

Definitely a little bit too smug. "I simply don't need my sister poking her nose into my business."

As she watched him leave, Christina had to forcefully remind herself to close her mouth and not stare after him like a fool.

But it was difficult to do.

After all, today was the first day she could ever remember hearing him call her his sister.

And now that she had heard it? She didn't care for the sound of it. Not one bit.

I hope everyone won't be too shocked when we tell them our news, Ben," Judith said as they walked toward the front door of her parents' house.

"Oh, they're going to be shocked," Ben replied in that confident way of his. "And they're going to have lots to say, too."

"You think so?" They really didn't have time for a long, involved discussion. There were too many things to do!

"I'm certain of it. This is your family, after all. Everything is cause for commotion, discussion, and excitement."

Thinking of the many big events . . . and the many more small ones that only felt big, Judith sighed. Usually, she didn't mind everyone's exuberance. She liked how their excitement made even the most mundane of things feel like something special.

But now, well, she wasn't sure that she herself was ready to be in the middle of a Graber family hurricane. "I fear you are right."

Ben gripped her shoulder as he rapped twice on the door before turning the knob. "Chin up, Judith," he whispered before guiding her inside.

"Who's here? Oh, Judith! And Ben?" Looking from one to

the other, her mother's voice faltered a bit. As did her steps. "This is a surprise. Is . . . Is everything all right?"

After smiling softly at Ben, Judith said, "Mamm, we have something to tell you. Do you have time to talk?"

"Of course I do." A line appeared between her brows as she gazed from Ben to Judith to Ben again. "What has happened?"

"Something exciting. And scary, too."

"Scary, you say?"

"*Nee*, I mean . . . I mean. . . . Oh, I don't know what I mean." Feeling tongue-tied and helpless, she turned to Ben. Silently pleading for his help.

He came to the rescue just as she'd hoped. "What my *frau* is trying to say is that we will be fostering a baby soon."

"Soon? How soon?"

"He'll be arriving tomorrow morning."

Her mother's eyebrows lifted so high, Judith almost feared they'd get lost in her hairline. But to her mother's credit, she simply smiled. "Well, now. Isn't that *gut* news? Come into the kitchen and tell us about it."

Us? Suddenly worried that her news was about to get sucked into the usual family whirlwind, Judith paused. "Who else is here?"

"You got lucky today, dear. There's only Clara, her babies, and Gretta. Everyone else is either working on the farm or at the store."

Feeling chagrined, Judith said, "Mamm, you know me so well it's almost as if you read my mind! I wasn't ready to have a big discussion with the whole family."

"I don't need to read your mind to know that you'd like a little bit of privacy to share such an important bit of news," she said as she led the way into the kitchen.

Once there, Judith and Ben greeted Gretta and Clara and

their babies, who were either sitting in high chairs or playing on a quilt on the floor. After kissing the children and exchanging greetings and accepting cups of coffee, Judith sat by Ben's side and explained everything that had happened during the last twenty-four hours. "It all started with a visit from Bernie, our social worker," she said.

Clara leaned forward. "And?"

"And she said there was a woman who had recently had a baby in prison."

Gretta blinked. "The mother is in prison?"

Judith couldn't fault Gretta's look of shock. But it was funny, because she realized she was starting to take that in stride now. "The baby's name is James."

The worried lines on her mother's forehead smoothed. "James, is it? Tell us more, dear."

And so Judith did. She told her all about Bernie's visit telling them what it meant to be foster parents. She told them about her prayers the night before and their phone call that morning. Finally, she revealed that baby James would be arriving the very next morning.

As she expected, the other women's expressions flickered between amazement, sadness for the mother behind bars, and a mixture of joy and doubt as Judith explained what she knew about fostering.

And then pure shock.

"Tomorrow morning you say?" her mother asked.

To Judith's relief, Ben answered that one. "We didn't want to wait. And frankly, Bernie didn't want to wait any longer, either. That's why we're here. We need your help."

For a few seconds, the only noise in the room was Clara's twins cooing to each other. Then, Gretta spoke. "I am mighty happy for you, Judith. What can I do?"

And wasn't that just like Gretta? Josh's wife was always quiet, always thoughtful. But most of all, she didn't spend a lot of time on dramatics. Instead, she always got to the heart of things. Her demeanor soothed Judith's nervous energy like little else could have.

"I need advice. And baby things. And . . . And I'm not even sure! I've helped babysit your *kinner*, but I fear that isn't the same thing."

Clara and Gretta looked at each other and chuckled. "It is certainly not," Clara said. "Oh, Judith, we are going to have a busy day!"

At last, her mother enfolded her in her arms and hugged her tightly. "But not to worry. We're going to get it all done."

"You really think it's possible?"

"But of course! I promise, dear, you came to the right place. Now, let's make some lists and start sending our men to various houses to gather things."

"You're simply going to send the men out on your errands?" Ben joked.

"Oh, *jah*," her mother replied with a new gleam in her eye. "Here's my first command. Benjamin, go to the barn and tell Tim and Anson to come inside right this minute. We have work to do."

"I'm on my way." After squeezing Judith's hand, he left the kitchen like he'd just been given a vacation.

Once the door closed, her mother got out a pencil and paper and handed it to Judith. "Daughter, get ready. You're about to get more advice than you'll know what to do with."

"I'm ready, Mamm." Yes, she was more than ready for anything. She was sure of it.

chapter six

"Where did you hide your smile today?" Mrs. Kent asked Christina when she entered the Sugarcreek Inn the following morning. "I usually never see you without it."

"I'm afraid I don't have too much to smile about this morning," Christina said.

Looking concerned, Jana put down the menu she was wiping and walked to her side. "What's wrong? Is someone sick?"

"*Nee.* It's nothing like that." Christina tried to smile, but she feared that instead of looking happy she looked more like she was heading to a funeral. "It's just been a challenging twenty-four hours."

"Would you like to talk about it?" Jana gestured around the dining room. "We're not too busy, I'd be happy to listen."

It was gestures like this that made her feel so blessed to be working at the Sugarcreek Inn. Sure, the work was hard, but Mrs. Kent truly did care about each of her employees.

But not even a kind heart and a willingness to listen were going to ease her worries. "*Danke*, but it's nothing too serious. I'm simply a little upset about something that's going on at home." With effort, she shook off her mood. "I promise, I'll be better in a minute. I'm sorry for bringing my blue mood to work."

"You don't need to apologize. I'm afraid I've given you all a share of my moods a time or two. Especially lately."

All of the employees had been aware that their boss had been more impatient and grumpy than usual. Just the week before, Ruth had secretly grumbled that she was tempted to march into their boss's office and send her home for the day!

But Christina figured it would be best not to say a word about that. "So, what would you like me to do today? Dishes?" Ironically, she realized she wouldn't mind even if her boss wanted her to wash dishes all day. At least then she wouldn't have to say a word to anyone. If she was standing in front of the sink, she could stew to her heart's content.

"No dishes for you. Jolene is doing a great job with them. Actually, I scheduled you to be a server again today. How does that sound?"

Well, there was only one answer to that. "It sounds *gut*. I'll go put a white apron on."

"Whatever it is that's bothering you, I hope it passes soon, dear."

"*Danke*, Jana." Realizing she was about to start crying yet again, Christina hurried to the kitchen. After quietly greeting Marla and Ruth, she slipped a white apron on and then headed back to the dining room.

Just in time to greet a table of four that Jana had just seated. "*Gut matin*," she said politely. "May I bring you a cup of *kaffi* or some juice?"

"I'll take a cup," a deep voice murmured.

She met the customer's gaze. And then nearly dropped her pencil. He had lovely eyes, dark green with faint flecks of gold in them. And those eyes were gazing at her in an appreciative way.

When she realized she had stared right back at him for a full second, she blurted, "Do you take cream?"

His expression remained solemn, as if she'd just asked him

the most important question in the world. But then his lips turned up. *"Nee."*

To her amazement, her insides gave a little jump. And before she quite realized what she was about, she found herself smiling right back at him.

He chuckled. "I was wondering if you were ever going to smile."

"I'm sorry. I . . . I'm distracted this mornin'." Kind of like she was feeling distracted right at that moment.

"My wife and I would also like some *kaffi*, miss," another man, who could only be the man's father, gently reminded her. "And my daughter would like some hot chocolate."

Christina felt her cheeks flush. "Oh! Oh, *jah*. To be sure. I mean . . . all right. I mean, I'll be right back with a carafe. In a moment."

The moment she turned around, she closed her eyes in mortification. She sounded as ditzy as a thirteen-year-old around her first crush! Stepping away, she made a point to breathe deeply and get her bearings.

When she returned moments later, she found herself meeting that man's gaze again as she poured his coffee. After also filling his parents' mugs, and delivering the girl's hot chocolate, and taking their orders. And yet again when she delivered their food.

Even when she was waiting on other tables, she found herself glancing his way. When the boy's mother raised her eyebrows at Christina, she felt herself blush. She surely was making a cake of herself. For sure and for certain!

She'd just brought dessert to a trio of English ladies who were visiting from Michigan when the family got up to leave.

Christina breathed a sigh of relief. It had been almost impossible to concentrate on anything while they'd been there.

"*Danke* for coming in," she said politely, just like Jana had taught her. "I hope you will come back soon."

He stayed behind after his family filed out. "If I come back, will I have a good chance of seeing you?"

"You will if I'm working," she teased.

"What days do you work?"

"Almost every day."

A dimple appeared. "Which means?"

Though he was being a tad bit forward, she couldn't deny that she was flattered. "I work mornings on Monday through Thursday. Some Saturdays, too."

"So, if I come in, and you happened to see me . . . Would you make time to talk to me?"

Christina gulped. Her sister Treva would have played hard to get. Her mother would have told her to ignore him completely. But she didn't have any desire to play games. "If you do come in, and I happen to see you . . . yes, I will talk to you," she said with a small smile.

"I'll see you one day very soon, then."

She nodded stupidly as she watched him leave, only realizing after he and his family left that she didn't even know his name.

And that for the first time in days, she'd hardly spared Aden Reese a thought.

"Who was that?" Jana asked as she walked to Christina's side. "He sure is cute."

"I don't know."

"Really? It looked like you two were chatting just a second ago."

"We were. Um, he asked about my schedule, saying he planned to come in soon." Impulsively, she said, "He said he wants to see me."

Jana chuckled softly. "That would make any girl's day, I think. He was very handsome. And if you don't mind me saying so, it looked like he only had eyes for you."

It certainly had felt like that. "He was nice." Realizing she was standing there like a statue, she shook herself out of her reverie. "I'd best get busy."

As she walked away, Christina wondered if the Lord had decided to shine on her a bit that morning. Here she'd been so upset, thinking about Aden leaving her. And so jealous, thinking that he'd found someone to court.

But maybe the Lord had brought this boy in the restaurant as a reminder that there were a lot of other men out there. A lot more fish in the sea, as her mother liked to say.

And if that was the case? Well, that was a mighty nice thing to remember. For sure and for certain.

As she walked back to her office, Jana couldn't help smiling. That Christina was as cute as a button. Seeing her shyly flirting with that young man made her think of younger days.

And how time flew.

Once in her office, she closed her door and leaned back in her chair. Almost at once, her eyes fastened on an old family photo, one they'd hired a professional photographer to take in front of their house.

Oh, but they'd all loved that house. She and Harrison had worked with a builder for two full years to get the Victorian design just right. It had a wraparound porch, a three-season room, and three fireplaces. The back of it faced the woods, offering her some valued privacy, but it also was nestled in the middle of a street, giving her four children plenty of friends to play with.

Those had been such happy years.

Then Harrison had gotten sick. Too soon after that, she'd been a widow with four teenagers.

Life had moved on, and one by one, they'd all gone off to college. At least once a month she would wonder why she hadn't moved. But then she would think of the children. Naturally, they'd clung to that house and the memories that had been made there. Whenever they all returned home on college breaks or the occasional weekend, they'd been excited for everything to be how it used to be. For a few days, the big house would be filled with happy noises, piles of laundry, and sporting equipment and a hundred other things that her kids had procured.

Sometimes, it had been like old times. Well, almost.

Of course, what the kids had neglected to realize was that when they left, the old house went back to being too big and too much to take care of. Instead of feeling like her escape from the world, the house became a place to clean and fix and rattle around in.

And a place to hold on to memories. Which were lovely, but also painful. It was hard to look at Harrison's empty side of the closet without remembering all his suits hanging there. Or his favorite spot in their living room—the old chair that had been always surrounded with newspapers and magazines.

So, after much deliberation, she'd put it up for sale. As she'd expected, the change hadn't gone over real well with the kids. It didn't seem to matter that they no longer lived there. . . . They wanted things from their past to stay the same. It took quite a lot of convincing and no small amount of tears to remind the children that nothing stayed the same for very long.

Within two months, her home sold. In exchange, she'd

bought a small little bungalow in the old section of Sugarcreek. The kids took some of the extra furniture, she sold the rest, and finally, on a rainy day in May, she moved into her new home.

There, living in the two-bedroom home with its tiny garden patio and antique bathroom with the claw-footed bathtub, she'd felt like she'd finally made a change in her life.

Now, sitting alone in her office, she knew it was time for another change.

Her recent evening at Pippa's had much to do with her decision . . . as well as the visit before with the accountant. The Sugarcreek Inn had become a money pit. If she wasn't careful, she was going to put her retirement in jeopardy—all in an effort to keep a restaurant she was tired of devoting so much of her time to to keep afloat.

"You need a partner," Pippa had said.

To her surprise, Jana didn't reject the idea immediately. Having someone to share both the financial burdens and the grueling schedule with would be a blessing indeed. "How do you think that would work?"

"All you have to do is find someone who wants to get into the restaurant business but wants to get in slowly. Then, little by little, this new partner can work more and more while you work less and less."

It sounded very intriguing. But she'd lived long enough to know such things didn't happen so easily. "And how do you think that would happen?" she'd asked, her voice a bit sarcastic. "We'd have to actually find someone who wanted to be a part owner in an Amish restaurant in Sugarcreek. I don't want to sound completely negative, but Sugarcreek isn't exactly a bustling metropolis."

"It only takes one person to want to go into business with you, Jana."

"That is true. But even finding one person might be—"

Pippa interrupted. "Jana, I'm talking about me."

"You?"

To Jana's chagrin, Pippa looked hurt. "Why not me?"

Jana knew she should tread carefully. Pippa was young—well younger. And therefore she, no doubt, had a lot of dreams that shouldn't be squashed.

But the girl probably had no idea of the amount of money and time that was involved. Not wanting to hurt her feelings, she decided to go slowly. "Well, for starters, I didn't think you especially liked Amish food."

"I like it. I was in the restaurant this week, remember? I got a vegetable plate."

"And . . . I don't want to sound rude, but I have a feeling that the amount to buy into a partnership would be a lot of money." Jana felt terrible. She didn't want to state the obvious, but well, Pippa was working at the Walmart and she lived in a small one-bedroom apartment. . . .

Pippa raised her chin. "I have money in savings, Jana. A lot of money. Just because I haven't spent it doesn't mean it's not there." As Jana processed that, Pippa continued, her voice turning excited. "And I like working at Walmart. I was working there until I figured out what I wanted to do."

Pippa took a deep breath and glared at Jana. "It wasn't because I couldn't get a job anyplace else."

Now she felt even worse. "Of course. I'm sorry—"

"I happen to think I would be a good fit. We enjoy being together, and I don't mind working. I'm also a quick learner. And I get along with people, too."

"Yes," she murmured helplessly. It was becoming obvious that Pippa had done a lot of thinking about this.

"Just think about it, will you? I have a feeling some of your patrons might enjoy a plate of enchiladas with their chicken every once in a while."

Jana had been horrified. She did not intend to ever serve Mexican food alongside Amish pies and traditional fare. But she was unwilling to hurt her friend's feelings any more so she held her tongue.

But now, here she was, thinking about freedom and the future. And, to her surprise, she was even wondering if her customers might like the chance to eat Mexican food every once in a while at the Sugarcreek Inn.

Maybe they would!

And furthermore, maybe it wasn't even her decision. What would be so wrong about offering the choice? If customers didn't care for the Mexican choices they would let Pippa know.

So . . . now what?

The possibilities of what to do next felt endless. She could seriously consider Pippa's suggestion or let other folks in the business community know she was looking for a partner.

Or she could keep things exactly the same.

Feeling a bit confused and even more despondent, she picked up the phone and called Melissa, her youngest daughter.

She picked up on the first ring. "Hey, Mom. What's up?" she asked in that easy, breezy way of hers.

"Nothing much. I was just thinking about you. How are things in the city?"

"Cleveland's about like it always is," she said with a laugh. "The hotel has been really busy. We had a corporate dinner and a wedding yesterday. Every room has been booked for the last week."

Melissa worked for one of the big, fancy hotel chains in downtown Cleveland. She had some kind of job title that was just as fancy, too. Something to do with special events. Jana was so proud of her. Melissa had once been her little list maker. Now she was putting all her organizational gifts to good use.

"My goodness. I can't wait to hear all about it."

"I have some good stories, too. I'll tell them to you when we see each other next."

Jana grinned. Here was the opening she'd been looking for! "That's the exact reason I called, Mel. I was thinking that maybe you could come home soon. It's been too long since I've seen you."

"You're right. It has been a long time. Weeks."

"I haven't seen you since Christmas Day," Jana reminded her. "Want to come out this weekend? You know how the cold never bothered us. We can go for a nice long walk like we used to."

After a pause, Melissa's voice turned concerned. "What's wrong, Mom?"

"Not a thing."

"Are you sure?"

Jana felt embarrassed now. Was she so transparent, so needy, that Melissa could tell something was wrong in just a few minutes? "I didn't think I needed a reason to invite you to come home."

"Of course not. I'm sorry, Mom."

Of course not, followed by a quick apology. Jana realized with a bit of surprise that she had said almost the same words to Pippa when she was backpedaling. "So, do you think you could come down soon?"

"Gee, I don't know, Mom. Things are pretty busy right now. Every weekend is booked with either weddings or celebrities coming in for the Rock and Roll Museum."

"You don't have anyone to help you?"

"I do, but these events are my responsibility. I can't put them on someone else. This is my job, Mom."

Jana noticed that Melissa didn't ask her to come visit her instead. It was hard, but she pushed her disappointment to one side. "I understand."

Another long pause. "Mom, do you want me to call Jane to see if she has some free time?"

Jane. The child who liked to think she could take care of everything, anytime, anyplace. "I can call Jane myself."

"All right." After an awkward pause, Melissa said, "Um, listen, my email is going crazy. I have to get some things done before my ten o'clock appointment."

Swallowing her disappointment, Jana let Melissa go. "Sure, honey. I'll call you again very soon."

"Okay. Great. Thanks, Mom. Love you!"

Melissa clicked off before Jana could tell her the same thing. Feeling a bit at loose ends, she stood up and stretched her arms. It was time to get back to work.

But it was also past time to make a change. She needed to call Pippa and accept her offer.

The sooner the better.

chapter seven

Judith's palms were damp. Hastily—and for about the tenth time in the last hour—she wiped them on the skirt of her raspberry-colored dress. "Ben, would you think me awful if I told ya I was scared to death?"

"I'd feel relieved. I kind of feel like I'm about to throw up."

"You feel that good?" she teased.

He grinned. "I guess that sounded pretty bad. It's just my stomach is a bundle of nerves. And I kind of feel like I'm in a daze, too. Almost like I'm in a dream and I'm about to wake up."

"That's how I feel. I'm scared and nervous and impatient and excited."

"I can't believe we're standing here on the porch wait-ing for Bernie and James to arrive." Fingering the blue wool shawl she'd thrown over her shoulders, he looked at her with concern. "Are you sure you're not too cold? It is January, you know."

"I'm not cold at all. The sun is out. It's a beautiful day, especially for January. Besides, there was no way I could stay inside. I was practically wearing a hole on the rag rug in the front room!"

"I'm glad we're standing out here, too. I can't seem to do anything but look out onto the street, and I sure didn't want to stand inside with my nose pressed to the window."

Once again Judith couldn't believe how lucky she was to have Ben for her husband. He'd been nothing but supportive during the past year. He'd celebrated with her when she'd discovered she was pregnant and had held her for hours and hours after she'd had the miscarriage. He'd vowed it didn't matter to him after they discovered she couldn't get pregnant again. It had been his idea to fill out the paperwork for adoption. And now he was as eager to be a foster parent as she was.

"Ben, have I told you that I love you today?"

To her pleasure, he rested a heavy hand on her shoulder. "Only today?"

"Oh, I love you every day. But I love you *especially* today."

As she'd hoped, he grinned. "And what made you say that, dear wife?"

"Because I wouldn't want to do this with anyone else," she said lightly.

"I agree. I don't think I could get through this with anyone else. You are a wonderful *frau*, Judith. And once more, you're going to be a wonderful mother."

"I hope so."

"I know you will be." He took a breath, obviously about to say something else, but then his expression froze.

Feeling frozen herself, she turned her head and looked in the same direction. And saw that their big moment had indeed come. Bernie and James had arrived.

The social worker barely had time to park her sedan before Judith scampered down the three steps to meet them. Ben followed, but at a much slower—and more hesitant—pace.

The moment the social worker opened her door, Judith felt her eyes swim with tears. "Hi, Bernie."

"Good morning, you two. Are you ready for your big day?"

"As ready as we'll ever be," Ben said with a grin.

Bernie's blond hair was in a ponytail today and her ever-present reading glasses were perched on the top of her head. "You two look like you're ready for Christmas Day," she teased.

"I feel like it is Christmas," Judith remarked as she watched Bernie open the door and reach inside, unbuckle a small bundle from the car seat, and at last bring out a tiny baby. Baby James.

Holding the quiet baby, who was wrapped in a soft-looking plaid flannel blanket, close to her chest, Bernie straightened and met Judith's gaze. "Judith, this is James," she said with a soft smile.

Heart pounding, Judith reached out to the newborn. Carefully cradling his head like her sister-in-law had reminded her to do, she felt tears prick her eyes. He was so light! So small! Closing her eyes, she cuddled him close, taking in his scent.

"Oh, James," she murmured. "I'm so *verra* glad you are here." Looking down at his face, she smiled softly. Then froze.

The baby had brown skin.

"The baby is African American," she exclaimed in surprise.

Bernie's eyebrows rose. "Ah, yes. Yes, he is." Then, as if she heard something she hadn't expected in Judith's tone, she stepped closer. Almost as if she was ready to take back James. "I thought I'd mentioned it, but to tell you the truth, I didn't think it mattered."

All Judith could think was that now no one would ever look at her and James and think that the baby was hers. "You didn't tell me that he wouldn't be white."

"Again, I didn't think it mattered." Looking from Judith to Ben, Bernie's voice turned even more protective. "Is this a problem?"

Judith wasn't sure. No matter how much Bernie had explained to her about fostering a child, or how much Ben had reminded her that becoming a foster parent was only a temporary thing, Judith had secretly held a few dreams in her heart. She'd imagined having an instant bond with the baby.

She'd hoped that one day the baby's mother might want her and Ben to be James's forever parents. And then, very secretly, she imagined raising the boy as their own. She'd even imagined that eventually everyone would forget that the baby wasn't theirs by blood. He would stop being the foster baby and would simply become James Knox.

But this baby looked so different from her! No one would ever believe he'd been hers since birth.

"Of course it doesn't matter what he looks like. This ain't a problem. Not a problem at all," Ben said quickly. "We feel blessed to have this time with James. Isn't that right, Judith?"

"Oh, *jah*. Yes, of course."

Ben looked at Judith strangely as he stepped in front of her and reached for the tiny baby. "Judith, may I hold him now?"

Still feeling like she was in a daze, she handed James to Ben. James settled easily into her husband's arms, all the while looking at her husband with wide brown eyes.

Ben smiled. "Look at that! Not a single tear from this little guy!"

Bernie reached out and gently ran a finger along James's chubby cheek. "I have to tell you, he is one of the sweetest babies I've ever had the honor of helping. He's got a wonderful disposition. So easygoing."

"He is going to be a joy to have around," Ben murmured. Then he raised his head and stared hard at Judith. "Don't you agree, Judith?"

His look finally served to push her from her daze. "Hmm?

Oh, *jah*. I mean, yes, of course." She stepped to her husband's side and looked down at James. "He is a sweetie, isn't he," she said with a smile.

Reaching out, she gently rubbed the tiny hand that had popped out of the plaid blanket.

James turned his head and met her gaze. And then, to her surprise, grabbed ahold of her finger.

"Oh! Oh, look at that, Ben!"

"I think he's telling you something," Ben teased.

Staring into James's eyes, feeling his little hand wrapped around her finger, she realized that he'd just wrapped himself around her heart, too. And just like that, she felt every stitch of worry and doubt and, well, ridiculousness fade away.

There in her husband's arms was the most beautiful baby in the world. And she knew in that instant that they were meant to be together.

Lifting her arms out, she smiled at them both. "May I have him back now?"

Ben's expression eased and something soft and sweet entered his eyes. "Of course, dear. Here you go. Mind his head, now."

She rested one hand on the back of James's soft, curly head and carefully eased him into her arms. And as the baby easily cuddled closer, making a little noise of what she could only imagine was happiness, Judith finally understood what it meant to love without reservations. Her love for this little boy was limitless.

Bernie clasped her hands together. "I knew this was the right decision," she stated, satisfaction in her tone. "Look at you three. Already, you look like a family."

The tears that had threatened to fall all morning at last fell down her cheeks. "We are so thankful for him, Bernie."

Then she shifted James so she could look at his sweet little face once again. "I am so thankful for you, James. You are truly God's gift. All *kinner* are."

I heard through the grapevine that you're going to be moving out on your own, Aden," Junior Beiler mentioned when their paths crossed outside the Graber Country Store just before suppertime.

"News travels fast."

Junior chuckled. "Good news does. It is good news, right?"

"Definitely. I'm actually looking forward to living in town."

"Have you found an apartment yet?"

"Nope." After peeking to make sure that no one they knew could overhear, Aden added, "I feel kind of foolish. I have some money saved up, but obviously not as much as most places want. I hadn't realized everyone was going to be wanting both my first and last month's rent. And a security deposit."

"It all adds up, for sure."

"I guess I'm going to have to set my sights a little lower."

"Now that the economy is turning around, I heard some of the places have raised their prices."

"That makes sense. I just wish they weren't raising them quite as much as they are," Aden declared as Miriam, Junior's new wife approached. "Hi there, Miriam."

After smiling at Junior in a very sweet way, Miriam turned to him. "Hi, Aden. How are you?"

"I'm good. Just talking to your husband before I run over to the restaurant to pick up Christina."

"Tell her hello for me. I miss seeing her every day."

"I'll tell her. I know she misses seeing you." Until recently,

Miriam had worked at the Sugarcreek Inn. She'd worked there a good five years. Aden recalled Christina saying once that many thought of Miriam as being the heart and soul of the inn.

"Aden is out looking for an apartment in Sugarcreek."

"For who?"

"Me. I thought it was time to get a place of my own."

"Why?"

Junior winced. "Miriam, you can't ask him something like that. His reasons aren't any of our concern."

She instantly looked abashed. "I'm sorry. I was only thinking your situation was a lot like Junior's here. You both are the eldest boys in a big household."

"My situation isn't quite the same. I'm not really a part of the Kempf family, you know. They've only been kind enough to take me in for years."

Miriam raised her brows. "I don't know that they ever thought of you as an inconvenience. Christina always acted like she was pleased as punch that you were living there."

"Well, Christina is . . . um, older now."

"Yes, that is true. But—"

Junior cut her off. "Miriam, I just thought of something. What do you know about Mary Kate's old apartment?"

"The apartment over the old hardware store? It's still vacant, I think." She brightened. "Oh, that would be a *wonderful-gut* spot for you, Aden. It's close to everything."

"And because the owners are anxious to have it filled, it might be going for a good price. Especially given its history and all," Junior added. "Who knows? Maybe they'll even work with you on the first and last month's rent."

"If that's the case it would be a real blessing." Aden knew that one of Miriam's best friends had lived in that apartment, but her ex-boyfriend had shown up there and attacked her. It had created a ruckus in town. He'd even heard some of the more superstitious people in town were certain that the place was cursed and didn't want anything to do with it.

Junior eyed him closely. "You know about its history, right? Would you find it difficult to live there? Some folks do."

"Not at all." It was going to take a whole lot more than another couple's fight to have him turn away a place that might be going for an affordable price. "I'll go down to the bank tomorrow and ask who I can talk to about it."

"I hope it all works out," Miriam said. "The last time I talked with Mary Kate, she said she felt real bad that she'd broken her lease so suddenly."

"After you get everything ironed out, be sure to let me know if you need help moving," Junior piped in. "My brothers and I will be glad to lend a hand."

"*Danke.* I'll let you know what happens."

With a worried look at the sky, Junior said, "Now I better get Miriam home. Mr. Graber told us that snow is on the way."

After wishing them both a good evening, Aden walked briskly to the Sugarcreek Inn. If Mr. Graber was right—and he was always right about snow—he was going to have just enough time to grab a slice of pie before it was time to head back to the Kempfs' farm.

chapter eight

It took a bit of effort, but Christina was discovering if she really concentrated, she could act as if seeing Aden at the end of a very long day was nothing special. Nothing special at all.

Over and over again, she reminded herself about how flattered she had been when the man with the striking green eyes had flirted with her earlier that day. Though she might never see him again, he was serving as a good reminder that Aden Reese was not the only fish in the sea.

She needed to keep reminding herself that Aden was moving forward with his life. He had a job at the hospital, was looking for a place of his own, and was even interested in another woman.

She was going to get her heart broken if she continually held out hope that Aden Reese was going to fall in love with her one day.

Doing her best to seem nonchalant, she placed a large slice of pie down in front of him. "You're a lucky man, Aden. This was our last slice of lemon meringue."

"It's my lucky day, to be sure." After he picked up his fork, he looked at her with a frown. "Aren't you going to sit down and join me?"

If she sat down, she'd be tempted to start chatting. Possibly even smile. And then there would go her best intentions! "I'm afraid I can't today. I'm pretty busy, you see."

He looked around the half-empty restaurant. "Really? Doing what?"

"Um, I'm needed in the kitchen." She backed up a step to prove her point.

Down went that fork. "But your day is done, right? Or is Mrs. Kent making you work late?"

The very last thing she needed was for Aden to get on his high horse and start asking Mrs. Kent if Christina was getting her overtime. "*Nee* . . . it's just something personal I have to take care of."

But instead of looking satisfied with her excuse he merely looked a little more concerned. "Something personal? Is something wrong?"

"Not with me. It's with Ruth. She's having some family problems."

"I hope it's nothing serious."

"I hope not, too. But I did promise her that we'd talk before I left. I'll be right back."

And with that, she scurried to the kitchen. Only as she practically trotted through the swinging doors did she realize that Ruth was following right on her heels.

Which brought her up short. "Ruth, you scared me!"

"You scared me a bit, too, if you want to know the truth. It's not every day I overhear that I'm having family issues."

"Sorry about that."

Ruth's eyes sparkled as she wrapped an arm around Christina's shoulders. "Care to explain what has been going on in your head?"

"I just made that up so I wouldn't have to sit with Aden."

Ruth chuckled. "Well, next time you come up with a lie you might try looking around you first. I was standing right there."

Christina peeked out through the crack in the doors. "Oh . . . Oh . . . shoot. Do you think Aden noticed that you were in the dining room, too?"

Ruth's lips twitched. "Since he's not blind, I would say so," she quipped.

"Oh, but this is terrible."

The older woman rested her hands on her hips, stared at her hard, then grabbed Christina's hand and pulled her to the very back of the kitchen. Only when they were standing in the middle of the cubby where their coats and such hung, did Ruth let go of her hand. "I'll play along . . . if you tell me what's going on."

There was no reason to lie. Not to Ruth, who had children Christina's age. Ruth also had a habit of speaking bluntly and to the point. Miriam had used to say that their English friend could spot a lie from a mile away. "It's nothing. I'm simply trying to keep away from Aden."

Ruth narrowed her eyes. "That would make perfect sense, except that you two live in the same house. And he is here to pick you up. You planning to avoid him in that buggy of yours?"

Christina frowned at her friend's sarcastic tone. "I know we need to ride together. But I'm hoping to not visit with him if I don't have to."

"Because?"

"Because things with us are really messed up."

"You're talking in circles, Christina. You're going to have to be a bit clearer if you want my help."

"I don't know if I can. It's complicated."

A new thread of compassion eased into Ruth's voice. "Oh, my dear. You really are in a state. Why don't ya start slow? You obviously need to talk about this. It might as well be me."

Ruth had a point. "Well . . . " Her voice suddenly felt stuck in her throat. Because, she ached to say, she was hopeless. Hopelessly in love with him. Hopeless about having any kind of future with him, which was making her terribly sad. "Ruth, you might not know this, but I've liked Aden for a really long time," she finally blurted. "For years I've been waiting for him to realize I was grown up."

"Well, you're grown up now. And you're not only beautiful, but you're lovely on the inside, too. What's the problem?"

"He only sees me as his friend. And to make matters worse, he is moving out of our *haus*."

"Where is he going?"

"Somewhere in town. And it gets worse, too. He told me last night that he's also seeing a woman. He's dating an Englisher who he met at work," she sputtered. "At his hospital. Ruth, I think I've lost him before I even got a chance!"

Ruth winced. "Ouch. That has to be hard."

"You have no idea," Christina said. "Everything between us has changed now, and I'm so sad about it, too. I have a feeling that now, every time I look at Aden, I'm going to realize that everything I had thought we could have is never going to happen."

"Come now. It still might. . . . "

"And it also might not."

"Only the Lord knows our futures, dear. It seems to me that you're overthinking things. Perhaps you should start simply taking things one day at a time."

"I tried that. Today I met a boy while I was waitressing. He seemed to like me. He said he was going to come back because he wants to see me again."

"See? Everything is going to be just fine."

"I thought it was . . . until I saw Aden. Now I know no one can hold a candle to him."

Ruth patted her back. "You poor thing."

It was so good to talk to someone who understood. "You're right, though, Ruth. Somehow, some way, I need to move on with my life. Maybe if I try really hard, I'll learn how to not love Aden anymore."

"Oh, honey. I just don't know if it's that easy. Love doesn't work like that."

"I'm really hoping it's possible, though. It needs to."

A slight cough interrupted them. Christina spun around and came face-to-face with Pippa Reyes, Mrs. Kent's friend, standing in the doorway of Mrs. Kent's office.

Within seconds, Christina's face felt hot and she knew it was beet red. "I'm sorry. Were we disturbing you?"

Pippa shook her head. "Not at all. I, um, just couldn't help but overhear your conversation."

"I'm so sorry!" Wringing her hands together, Christina said, "I'm off the clock."

To Christina's surprise, Pippa's lips twitched. "No, it's not that. I, ah, just thought you should know I was standing here. I didn't want you to think I was meaning to eavesdrop on your private conversation. I'm not that way."

Ruth looked mildly embarrassed, too. "Pippa, I'm sorry, too. I know better than to encourage Christina to have such a private conversation in the kitchen." She paused, shifting her stance. "Um, since we're all standing here together, I wanted to tell you congratulations. Jana just told me that you are buying in to the business."

Pippa's smile grew. "Thank you, I'm really excited about working here with all of you."

Christina looked from Ruth to Pippa in confusion. "Wait a minute. Jana is leaving us?"

"Not at all," Pippa said, her dark brown eyes looking concerned. "Jana is simply ready to have some more free time. And I just happened to be looking for a better job."

"Oh." It all made sense. "Well, congratulations! And I'm sorry again about standing here whining about my love life."

"Your love life isn't any of my concern," Pippa protested with a wave of her hand. "But for what it's worth, it's been my experience that men don't always know what they want."

"Take it from me, they rarely know what they want," Ruth muttered.

Pippa's eyes twinkled. "Also, well . . . I've always felt that it was best to try not to worry about things you can't control. Give your worries over to the Lord. He's already got plans for you. He has plans for all of us."

Pippa's soft caring tone, combined with her heartfelt words eased Christina's worries. "*Danke.* That is *gut* advice."

"Thank you. Now, I hate to say it, but you ladies need to go on your way. It's starting to snow outside. The radio says we're due to get at least a foot by morning."

Ruth patted Christina's shoulders. "That is the best advice I've heard yet. If it's going to snow, I need to run to Graber's store and pick up some wood. And you, my dear, need to go get your cloak and find Aden. I'm betting he's wondering why you practically threw a plate of lemon pie at him and then darted off."

"I'll do that. Thank you both. I feel better," she added as she grabbed her cloak and walked back out to the dining room. To her surprise, Aden wasn't still sitting at his table. Instead, he had on his coat and hat and was pacing near the hostess table. The moment he saw her, he gave a sigh of relief.

"There you are," he said. "I was starting to think I was going to have to walk into the kitchen."

Making sure her pace was slow and her expression serene, Christina lifted her chin a bit. "I'm sorry. I had some things I needed to do."

"Is your friend Ruth all right?"

Feeling her cheeks heat, she said, "*Jah*. Now she is."

"Well, what happened?"

There was no way she was going to start trying to make up lies about Ruth. "It's a private thing. Between women, you know."

"You're sharing secrets that are that private? Isn't she fifty or something?"

"What difference does that make?"

Looking a little chastised, he shook his head. "Not a one, I suppose. Listen, the snow is really coming down. We need to leave now. Are you ready?"

"*Jah*. I am very ready."

Aden looked a bit confused by her hot and cold responses. But instead of saying anything more about it, he merely opened the door and gestured for her to pass.

Chin high, Christina walked ahead. Well, she'd managed to try Aden's patience in under five minutes. Obviously, learning to ignore Aden was going to take some getting used to.

As she glanced at him again, thinking about how handsome he looked, so tall and stalwart, she inwardly sighed.

It seemed it was going to take a little bit more practice than she'd previously thought.

By the time they'd walked to the buggy, the clouds were dark and thick overhead and it was snowing in earnest. After making sure Christina was inside the enclosure and settled, Aden unhitched Maisey.

To make matters worse, the sun had already started to set, meaning it would be almost dark by the time they got home. Aden frowned, realizing their journey home was going to take far longer than he'd anticipated, and it was going to be far more difficult, too. He hated driving the buggy in the snow.

And it looked like everyone on Main Street had been taken by surprise by the thick, sticky flakes. Cars were already sliding through intersections, their bright brake lights and irritable honking making Maisey even more tense.

It was obvious that no maintenance crews had treated the roads. They were going to be pretty hazardous very soon.

Well, that was just great. He had no blankets in the buggy and no flashlight, either.

Feeling upset with himself, he glanced at Christina. She was only wearing her light cloak and her black boots with the thin soles. "Do you have a heavier coat or mittens with you?"

"*Nee.*"

"Perfect." If their buggy got stuck or slid on the way home she would have a very difficult time walking anywhere.

Even though he knew he was getting ahead of himself, he started spinning all kinds of worst-case scenarios in his head. Imagining Christina getting sick or hurt.

"We should have left thirty minutes ago," he muttered. "Next time, be ready when I get there."

"Aden, I was ready. You were the one who wanted pie."

"I was done with my slice of pie in less than ten minutes. Then I had to wait another ten while you went gossiping with Ruth."

"I told you she had a personal problem. And I wasn't gone that long."

"And I'm telling you that we got out of the restaurant late and now we're havin' to drive this buggy out in the snow." He frowned. "It's really coming down now, too."

"The snow is not my doing, Aden."

"I didn't say it was."

"You're sure actin' like I'm inconveniencing you."

"All I'm saying is that this is going to be a difficult drive home."

"We've done it before," she pointed out.

"But you were better prepared."

He carefully reined in Maisey as traffic stalled, and felt Christina look over at him with a critical eye. "Aden, you don't look like you're dressed any warmer than me."

"That's different."

"Why? Because I'm a girl?"

Because she was Christina. "*Jah.* And because I promised your parents I'd see you safely home."

Something flashed in her eyes that looked a lot like hurt. "So that is why you're upset? Because you promised my parents that you'd look out for me?"

"Well, *jah.*" With effort he refrained from rolling his eyes. Christina knew as well as he did that Joe and Martha depended on him to keep her safe from harm.

He was able to glance at her just long enough to see her grit her teeth. "I'm only speaking the truth, Christy," he said.

"Well, just think, soon you won't have to make this drive anymore. You'll be living in town."

"Right now I'm feeling like it can't happen soon enough. Heaven help your brothers."

"My brothers are too young to come and get me! I'll simply be driving myself."

"You certainly won't."

"And why not?"

"Because it's not safe." At the moment, he didn't even care that they were verbally sparring like a pair of teenagers. She was able to get under his skin like no other. And she certainly knew how to get a rise out of him.

"Lots of women drive their own horse and buggy, Aden." She paused, then glared at him again. "Or maybe I'll even have someone else drive me around."

He hated these kinds of conversations, where they bickered like children. He was just about to tell her that, too.

But then what she said finally registered. "Who would you get to drive you home?"

"Another man. Maybe a beau."

Her comment startled him so much, he almost jerked on Maisey's reins. "What in the world does that mean?"

"About what you'd think." She had the nerve to sound all airy about it, too.

And that really gave him pause. "I didn't know you were seeing someone."

"I'm not yet. I mean, not exactly. But I'm hopeful that something is going to become of it."

"What do you mean by 'of it'? What have you done? And where did you meet him?"

"I don't see how that is any of your business, Aden."

"Christina," he bit out, wincing that his temper and worry had made him draw out her name to five syllables. But he couldn't help himself. She was making him crazy.

Well, imagining her with some mystery man was making him crazy.

"Don't you 'Christina' me. You know I'm right. You're moving away, Aden. You should stop worrying about me."

"You know I can't do that."

When they stopped again, he glanced at her. But this time he didn't gaze at her eyes. Instead, he let his gaze drift to her temple, to the faint scar along her hairline. The scar she'd gotten when she'd been struggling to get out of the ice all those years ago and the jagged edge of the ice had cut her delicate skin.

The scar had been deep enough that she probably had needed stitches, but her parents had decided to simply bandage it well. Now, whenever he looked at it, he remembered feeling helpless and scared to death.

And guilty.

"Are you staring at my scar again?" she snapped.

He'd had no idea she'd ever noticed that he'd done that. *"Nee."*

She folded her arms over her chest. "Aden Reese, one day you are going to have to let that accident go. Me falling into the ice was not your fault."

"Of course it was. I was older. I was supposed to look out for you."

"Why would you think that?"

"Why wouldn't I?"

"You didn't live with me. You were only my friend. No one asked you to watch over me."

He bit his tongue so he wouldn't say something dumb and admit how even back then he'd felt something special about her. Instead, he looked ahead, looked at the snow falling heavily, at the number of cars slipping and sliding on the slushy roads, and at the sun setting in the midst of it all.

"I think we need to go a back way home. I don't trust these

automobiles. And Maisey seems especially uneasy. I have a feeling she might get spooked."

And just like that, she became her usual sweet self again. "Of course. Whatever you think is best, Aden."

When he could, he veered the buggy right and directed Maisey down a far less congested road. That was good. The road was already a bit packed with snow, giving both Maisey's hooves and the buggy's wheels something easier to grip.

But it also was taking them a bit off their direct route. "We're going to be really late now. Maybe even an hour late."

"It will be okay."

"I don't want your parents to worry about you."

"My parents know I'm with you. And Aden, if they worry, they're going to worry about both of us," she said gently.

He knew what she meant. But he also knew that his role in the house was to take care of her. His muscles tensed as the wind picked up fifteen minutes later and the horse started having more difficulty pulling the buggy. "If it gets worse we might have to let Maisey loose and then walk home."

"I figured that."

After another ten minutes, he gave up the fight. "I don't want to hurt her. Will you be all right if we walk?"

"I'll be fine, Aden." Then, to his surprise, she reached over and gripped his hand. "I know you're worried about me getting hurt or sick, but you shouldn't."

"Of course I'm going to worry."

"Aden, listen to me. I'm not a little girl anymore," she said softly. "When you grew up, I did, too. Please stop thinking of me like I am a fragile, delicate child. I'm a grown woman."

She wasn't fragile; she was special. He knew the difference. But he also realized that she had a point. She was a grown woman—which was exactly why he was trying to move out of her house. "I know you're not a child. And I know you're not all that delicate. I just don't want anything to happen to you."

"Then it won't," she whispered. "We'll get through this together."

He hoped that was the case as he finally gave in to the reality of their situation, parked the buggy well off to the side of the road, and unhitched Maisey. Maisey was a smart horse and knew all the back roads around the farm better than any of them did. He knew she would make her way home across the fields in probably half the time that it would take him and Christina.

After making sure Christina was as bundled as possible, he steeled himself. "Let's go. With the Lord's help we should get back home within the hour."

"An hour's walk is nothing. A piece of cake," she joked.

Then just as he was searching for the right words to try to alleviate her worries, she turned and started walking at a brisk pace. Leading the way.

And for the first time in recent memory, he was content to follow.

chapter nine

Oh, but those first few hours with James had been a delight! An awkward, nerve-racking, wonderful delight!

Bernie had stayed with them for a full two hours, helping Judith and Ben change James's diaper, feeding him a bottle, and setting him down for a nap.

Judith was amazed by the social worker's ability to offer a helping hand while blending into the background. She'd only offered suggestions to Judith and Ben when they needed it—like when they had looked at her with wide, scared eyes when James had started crying loudly and they had been sure they'd done something terribly wrong.

"Babies cry because they can't talk," she said in her calm, easy way. "All you have to do is figure out what they want."

"But I don't know what he wants," Judith had whined.

"If he's just had a bottle, there's a good chance he needs to burp," Bernie said, then proceeded to show her what to do. And sure enough, after a few good pats, the baby had burped and then had promptly fallen asleep. As Bernie demonstrated, Judith chided herself—of course she knew that babies needed to be burped! She was just so nervous she had forgotten!

Ben had been mighty impressed, though. "Bernie, that's amazing."

"No, that's what babies do," she teased.

Then, just as Judith was starting to think that she and Ben and James needed a little time alone, Bernie stood up.

"I need to be on my way now, but I'll be sure to stop over again tomorrow."

"You don't mind?" Judith asked.

"Of course not! Seeing James happy here is going to be the best part of my day. Don't forget, you can call me tonight if you need something. But I have a feeling you three are going to do just fine."

"Thank you, Bernie. Thank you for trusting us with James," Judith said.

Bernie hugged her tight. "I never had any doubt you two would be just what this little guy needed," she said before walking out the door.

Ben peeked out the front window and chuckled. "She's already on her cell phone again. She's sure a busy lady."

"She's a *wonderful-gut* lady," Judith said as she gazed at James. "Ben, at last we're alone with our little baby."

"Our foster baby," Ben gently corrected.

"*Jah.* Of course I meant that."

For the next few hours, she and Ben hadn't done a single thing other than stare at James while he slept. The sight of the sweet baby in the crib in the corner of their bedroom had been a dream of hers for so long that enjoying the reality was a time too sweet to pass up.

Now, though, it was a different story. Judith's mother had just arrived, along with Gretta, Clara and Tim, and even Caleb and Rebecca. Only her father and Joshua were missing, since they were needed at the store.

And to Judith's dismay they were all staring at little James like he was a curiosity.

"I do wish all of you would stop looking at James like he's

any different from us. Why don't all of you go sit down and have a cup of *kaffi* while I hold him?" It was amazing how her motherly instincts had come out full force. In just a few hours, no less!

"Just because I was surprised that his skin was dark doesn't mean I don't think he's adorable, Judith," her mother chided. "You can't fault me for being surprised."

Though they were reacting just as she had, Judith felt more than a bit defensive. "Bernie said the only thing foster babies need is love and to be cared for. Ben and I can do that as well as anyone."

Her mother frowned. "We didn't say you couldn't, Judith."

Her brother Caleb had the audacity to roll his eyes. "Once again, you are making something out of nothing, Judith. Don't be so sensitive." And then he had the nerve to hold out his hands and say, "Now, pass me that baby. Rebecca and I want to hold him."

To her shame, she hugged James a little bit tighter. "He might not want you holding him. He's nervous around strangers."

"How do you know that?" Caleb asked. "You just met him yourself."

"We've bonded already. He likes me."

"If he doesn't like me, I'll give him back," Caleb said patiently. When she made no move to hand him the baby he glared, adding, "And don't you start telling me how we're not old enough to hold him. Rebecca's going to have our baby in just a few months' time."

"You can't fault his reasoning, Judith," Ben murmured. "Let Caleb hold James. You can't hold him all day and night, you know."

"I know." Carefully, she at last passed over James. "Don't forget about his head!"

Caleb said nothing, only raised his brows, then cuddled the baby closer and sat back down next to Rebecca. Within seconds, they were both cooing at James and he was looking back at them with a contented expression.

Judith wasn't sure if she was relieved that James was doing so well with them . . . or just a teeny bit jealous.

"It's going to be fine," Ben murmured.

"I just don't want to do anything wrong."

After gazing at her for a long minute, Ben said, "Would you men mind helping me look at one of the wheels on our buggy? It felt a little loose yesterday."

Looking relieved Tim and Caleb gathered their coats and tromped outside into the snow. Before leaving the room, Caleb passed James to their mother.

When it was only the women Gretta started giggling.

"What's so funny?"

"You are, Judith," Rebecca teased. "At the moment, I'm almost afraid of ya."

"I'm not that bad. . . ."

"Yes you are!" Gretta exclaimed. "My dear sister, you are a force to be reckoned with, for sure and for certain! I knew you would be a fierce mother hen, but you are even tougher than I thought you'd be."

Judith felt her cheeks heat. "Am I that bad?"

Clara looked at Rebecca, then said, "In a word? Yes."

"I'm sorry. I guess I'm just nervous."

"You wouldn't be my Judith if you weren't nervous." Her mother laughed. "Now, please sit down and relax, dear. We want to hear all about what your social worker said."

She sat on the edge of the couch. "All right. But, um, James might need his diaper changed. Or he might get hungry. . . ."

"If he does, we'll take care of it. Now please, dear, relax. Don't you see? Everything is okay."

In a burst of surprise, Judith realized her mother was right. Everything *was* okay. She needed to stop worrying and planning and fretting and take time to enjoy the moment. God was with them, and so was Ben and her family. And Bernie was only a phone call away. Why, there was practically a whole army of helping hands and hearts.

All she had to do was trust them. And maybe learn to trust herself a little bit, too.

"Well, first of all, Bernie said that James was born just a few days before Christmas. He's a Christmas baby!"

"A true miracle, to be sure," her mother murmured.

With a sigh, Judith finally relaxed and started chatting, letting all her enthusiasm show and all her worries fade to the wayside.

Everything was just fine. Why, it was obvious that she and James were meant to be together. Forever.

Jana was so glad Pippa had convinced her to take most of the afternoon and evening off. "I live just two blocks away," Pippa had reminded her. "If the snow gets worse, I'll simply close early and walk home."

"Okay. But if something goes wrong—"

"It won't."

"Don't forget, I'm just a phone call away if you need anything."

"I remember that. But I won't be calling you. I'll be fine." Playfully shaking a finger at her, Pippa said, "You better not call me, either."

"I'll try not to." Jana knew that wasn't the answer Pippa had wanted, but it was the best she could do. It was becoming apparent that it was going to take a bit of practice to learn how to relax.

For the past hour she'd attempted to read the same two pages of a novel, halfheartedly tried to organize the linen closet, and stared at the inside of a near-empty refrigerator. Annoyed with herself, she slipped on boots, mittens, and her cozy wool coat.

There was nothing like a walk in the snow to lift her spirits. And there was nowhere she'd rather walk to than the Grabers' store. She loved that place. It was the closest thing to an emporium in the area, and she never failed to find something interesting.

For the first time in, well, forever, she was actually going to have time to look at everything, too. The moment she entered the store and smelled the tantalizing combination of fresh balsam and cinnamon, she knew there was no better place to spend her free time.

Until she realized that she seemed to be the only contented person in the building. Three policemen were there, and Mr. Graber himself was standing by the door with an extremely put-upon expression on his face.

"Hiya, Jana."

"What's going on, Mr. Graber?"

"We've been robbed." Pointing to the three policemen wandering up and down the aisles with his son, Mr. Graber said, "I walked in this morning to find the front window broken, glass all over the floor, and all sorts of things missing . . . including four quilts."

She was shocked by the thought of such a crime happening in Sugarcreek. "This is terrible."

"*Jah*. We've had the store a *verra* long time. And in all these years, nothing like this ever occurred." He slumped a bit. "I have to admit that I'm a little bit at a loss of what to do. The police were gone, but now they're back." He rolled his eyes. "Still looking for clues or some such."

He looked so blue. "What can I do to help?"

"*Danke*, but there's nothing you can do. Unless you have any idea of who would do such a thing?"

"I'm sorry, I don't."

Mr. Graber slumped. "I figured as much. I guess we'll just have to clean up, then wait and see what happens. And hope the policemen here do their jobs."

"They will. We've got a great police department here."

"You're right about that. Well, I'd better go help our customers. Snow always means good business, you know."

Wondering how she could help, Jana glanced over at Adam Canfield, the chief of police. She knew him fairly well, thanks to his help when a couple of kids had decided to try their hand at dining and ditching.

Adam was about the age of her eldest son, Nick, and was even-tempered and unflappable. He was a good man, and ever since he'd given those teenagers a good talking-to, he'd become a frequent visitor to the Sugarcreek Inn with his wife and young son.

Adam was currently talking to Joshua Graber. But the other police officer was looking at her curiously. She figured the time was as right as any to introduce herself. "Hi. I'm Jana Kent. I own the Sugarcreek Inn. It's a restaurant just down the street."

The officer glanced at her like she'd interrupted his business. "Can I help you?"

"Maybe." She tried to smile. "I, ah, was just wondering if you had any idea who did this."

"Not yet." The expression in his eyes looked like it warred between impatience and amusement. "Usually it takes a bit longer than a couple of hours to solve a case."

His words, combined with the intense way he was looking at her, made her feel a little flustered—and wish that she'd thought to put on some lipstick. "No, I mean, is this the first robbery like this in Sugarcreek?"

"It's the first that I've heard about. I'll double-check with the other businesses on the street, though. Sometimes little things happen that no one takes the trouble to report."

"Thanks. That would be really nice of you."

"Anytime." He smiled politely, obviously ready for her to move on.

And she knew she should. But there was something about him that made her stand there just a little bit longer. "I don't think we've met. . . . Are you new?" When his brows rose, she rephrased her question. "I mean, are you new to Sugarcreek? I haven't seen you around before."

"I moved here two months ago. After putting in twenty years with the Akron P.D., I took a part-time job here." Somewhat dryly he added, "I'm supposedly transitioning into retirement."

Adam Canfield joined them. "Hey, Jana. Looks like you've met our new rookie?"

She laughed. "I'm bothering him, it's more like."

Officer Canfield smiled at the new officer, who looked old enough to be his father—or at least his uncle. "Jana, please meet Ross Capshaw. Ross, this is Jana Kent, owner of one of the best restaurants in town, the Sugarcreek Inn."

She waited for Ross to tell her friend that they'd just been talking. But instead, he held out his hand formally. "Nice to meet you, Mrs. Kent."

"Please, call me Jana. I'm not married." Immediately, she felt her cheeks heat. Why had she just said that? "Uh, I mean, I've been a widow for a long time now."

Officer Canfield's smile widened. Just fractionally, but enough to make Jana painfully aware that she was practically making a play for Sugarcreek's newest policeman right there in the middle of a robbery investigation.

Gosh, was that what she was doing?

Eager to sound more like she was making a friend than flirting, she said, "If you like pie, I hope you'll stop by." With a wink at Officer Canfield, she added, "Pie for police officers is always on the house. For their wives, too."

"Thank you," Ross said, his gaze warming slightly. "I just might do that. And it's just me. I'm not married, either."

She met his gaze again, felt that little tingle that she'd been sure had left her forever, and, well, stood there like she had nothing else to do.

"So, what are you thinking happened, Adam?" Mr. Graber said, joining them.

"It looks like some folks thought they needed some of your merchandise. And considering you don't have an alarm system, they might have gotten away with it all."

"We used to have Josh living up above here. And my daughter lived here for a time, but now no one does."

Adam frowned. "This is just my opinion, but I'm glad none of your family was here. Sometimes the burglars can be pretty desperate. I would have hated for one of your sons or daughters to have frightened them into doing something stupid."

"I am glad no one got hurt, of course. But this robbery is a *verra* bad thing for me." Mr. Graber's face fell. "I don't know what I'm going to tell those ladies who did all that quilting. Those quilts represented years of work, you know."

"Some of them were priced for over a thousand dollars," Jana said. "I'm really sorry."

"*Jah.* Me, too."

Ross looked at Mr. Graber with renewed interest. "Amish quilts can go for that much?"

"To be sure. They're hand quilted, you see. Real works of art."

"Do you have any photos of them? Has anyone taken pictures of them, do you know?"

"I'm not sure. We sure haven't. Why?"

"If we can find some photos, we might start hunting on the Internet. We've come across folks selling Amish goods on places like eBay and such."

Mr. Graber rubbed his long gray beard. "I'm going to have to do some thinking about this. I'll ask my *kinner* if they recall anyone taking photos of the quilts. A couple of tourists might have, I suppose. Or maybe an English friend of one of the quilters?"

"Come down and talk to us if you think of anything," Adam offered. "Either Ross or I will stop by here in a day or two to see how you're doing."

"*Danke.*"

As they finished their business, Jana took a step back, realizing all of a sudden that her lonely mood had lifted. There was nothing like someone else's problems to put your own into perspective.

Promising herself to return to check on the Grabers in a few days, she edged out the door.

"Jana?"

Surprised, she turned to find Ross following her. "Yes?"

"I ah, just wanted to say thanks for being so friendly. I'm sorry if I came across as a little gruff."

"You're the one who was working, Officer. You don't have to apologize for not having time to chat."

"It's Ross."

"Ross," she allowed, liking him more and more now that he wasn't acting quite so distant. She was also extremely pleased that now she wasn't the only one doing the talking. "I'm sure I came across as a bit of a busybody. I promise, that wasn't my intention. It's just that the Grabers are nice folks. They've helped me out more than a time or two over the years."

"I see that now. So, are you off to the restaurant right now?"

"I could be. May I offer you a piece of pie?" She smiled brightly. "Remember, it's on the house."

"I'd really like that. I mean, if you have time."

"I have time. My place is just down the street. And I am certain we have at least five kinds of pie just waiting for you to choose from. Coffee, too."

His chuckle was deep and gratifying. With lighter steps than she remembered having in years, she walked by his side in the falling snow. The flakes were thick and beautiful, rapidly coating everything with a clean white blanket.

It felt fresh and perfect. Lovely.

And suddenly Jana realized that the day had never been brighter.

chapter ten

Christina had lived in Sugarcreek all her life, and had happily spent much of it outside, enjoying their small-town life and peaceful surroundings. She'd run through wide fields dotted with wildflowers in the springtime, trudged home after bonfires in the autumn, and spent many a summer's evening watching birds with her Mommi. She had gloried in the late sunsets and taken many a moment to appreciate the beauty of a crystal-clear blue sky. She loved the area.

But no matter how hard she tried, she couldn't ever completely forget ten terrifying minutes spent on the skating pond when she was twelve years old. Since the accident, winter had become her least favorite season, and every time the temperature dropped, it brought back memories of shuddering in Aden's arms while he carried her home. Each year, when the air turned cold and all her friends and family were anxiously awaiting the first snow, she would retreat into herself.

She begged off from sledding and snowball fights and made sure she never had time to watch Treva try out her new ice skates. In short, she did her best to get through the winter, and did her best to get through it in silence, too. She was too embarrassed to have everyone know that she was still very affected by something that happened ten years ago.

Actually, no matter what season, she avoided the pond

like it held a monster in its depths. She could hardly look at any body of water without flinching.

And now, here it was in the distance, practically mocking her. Practically coaxing her to stop, burst into tears, and beg Aden to take care of her.

The weakness that threatened to ruin her independence was an irritation and a bother. And so many other things she didn't even have words for.

With each step closer to the pond, she took even more care to avoid looking at it. Anything to keep herself sane. "I see the farm in the distance," Christina said, taking care to interject a positive note into her voice, hoping Aden didn't hear the faint tremor that she couldn't quite hide. "It won't be much longer now."

Aden glanced her way, narrowed his eyes, then at last reached out, clasping her arm and pulling her to a stop. "Christina, being so close to this pond still scares you to death, doesn't it?"

She couldn't deny it. But she didn't want to dwell on it, either. "I'm fine."

"*Nee*. No, you are not."

She was trembling. But she preferred to imagine that her reaction was because she was exhausted. And cold. And anxious to sit down and eat about a gallon of soup. "I am well enough. Let's keep going, okay?"

His lips thinned, obviously finding fault with the way she was withholding the truth from him. "Christina, don't lie. Not to me." And although her chin was tucked and her face averted, he clasped his fingers around hers. "Does being near the pond still frighten you?"

His voice was gentle and tender. So tender that it was

tempting to admit just how bad her phobia was. But that wouldn't solve anything. "Nothing's wrong, Aden. I'm simply cold."

To her surprise, he didn't release her hand. Instead, he tugged her a little closer. "You're shaking."

"Because it's snowing—"

"*Nee*, that's not it." He moved a little more closely. Then, to her dismay, he clasped her other mittened hand. "What is it? Is it the memories? I didn't realize it bothered you so much after all this time."

"I'm not bothered."

"Liar."

Only Aden spoke to her like this. "All right. I am bothered. I don't like looking at the pond. That's all."

"Have you ever gone ice skating again? Have you ever gone over there in the winter? For the life of me, I can't remember."

She would give anything to not be having this discussion. "Aden, stop."

"You haven't, have you?" he pushed. "All this time, you've been keeping your fears to yourself."

To her shame, her eyes began to water. She hoped he wouldn't notice. She hated making him feel even more guilty.

But he still stared at her face. Then he lifted one of his gloved hands to her cheek and carefully wiped away a tear. "Talk to me, Christina."

"What is there to say?" With her own mittened hand she impatiently swiped at another tear that threatened to spill. "I am still afraid. So what?"

He turned his head and stared at the frozen pond in the distance. "So, it's been a long time, Christina. Ten years."

"I know. I can't explain it. I don't mind being near the water in the summer." *Not too much*, she silently added. "But when it's covered with ice, I can't bear to look at it."

"Oh, Christy." Very carefully, he cupped both hands around her shoulders, holding her so she had no choice but to face him.

And because she was essentially trapped, Christina looked into his eyes, mentally preparing herself for him to see the pain and the fear that was surely in the depths of hers.

As always, she found herself thinking what an unusual shade of brown his eyes were. And then she noticed how filled with tenderness they were. The emotion was so unguarded, so clear, it almost took her breath away.

Then he broke the moment. Letting go of her shoulders, he shoved his hands back into his pockets. "Come on," he said. "We're going to walk over there."

"*Nee!*" The word had been uttered loudly and with shame. But she couldn't help it. She felt as if he were hurting her.

Though, of course, he was doing no such thing.

Grasping her hand, he gave her a tug. "I promise, it will be all right. Come on."

He was too strong for her to pull away from his grasp. Too determined to listen to reason.

Her slight trembling increased tenfold as they drew closer. She clenched her teeth together so she wouldn't embarrass herself and start crying in earnest.

The border of the pond looked much as it had all those years ago. The far side was more built up, the side closer far more shallow. Four or five pine trees hugged the north side, where,in spring and summer, wildflowers and cattails decorated the edges, creating a home for all sorts of birds and animals.

But now all she saw was a thick snowbank looming directly in front of her. Just beyond it was the expanse of ice. The thick falling snow had blurred the lines between land and ice, between security and danger.

Though it made no sense, the closer they got to the ice, the more petrified she became. "Aden, I canna do this."

"You can. It's time, Christina."

She hated how assured he sounded. How confident. And how oblivious he was to her fear. "I can't believe you're making me stand here." She knew she was whining like a child, but she didn't care. At the moment she was willing to do whatever it took to save herself.

But Aden didn't seem bothered by her outbursts one bit. His face was set in a determined expression and his tone was as easy and calm as she'd ever heard it. "I promise, I'm not going to make you get any closer. All we're going to do is stand on the bank. No farther than that."

"Do you promise?"

"I promise."

"If you lie to me, I won't ever forgive you. I canna get on the ice, Aden."

"I won't make you do anything but stand at the edge. I promise, Christy. That's all." And with that, he tugged her three steps closer.

Though there was nothing in the air but snow, she felt her heartbeat quicken and her breathing turn shallow. She couldn't have said a word if she'd tried.

At last he stopped. They were just two small steps away from the frozen water.

If they'd knelt down, Christina knew she could place her palm on the ice. Simply imagining such a thing made her feel sick. She tried to close her eyes, but that only seemed to spur on the memories.

Aden slowly let go of her hand, then gently wrapped his arm around her shoulders. After the briefest of seconds, he gave her a reassuring squeeze. "Easy now," he murmured. "Look at you. You're doing real *gut*."

But she wasn't. Perspiration dotted her brow, and her hands were shaking. As each second passed like an hour, her barely attained control faltered.

Before even a full minute had passed, Christina jerked from Aden's strong clasp. "I'm sorry. I canna do this. Not anymore."

Then she turned and ran.

"Christina, hold on now."

Too afraid he was going to make her go back, she continued to run. In a panic, she scanned the area, looking for someplace safe to wait for him.

She hurried over to stand next to one of the trees. It made no sense, but she figured she could grab ahold of the tree if Aden tried to make her walk toward the edge again.

"Christina, I'm sorry," he called out. "I'm so sorry." After a pause, he walked over to stand beside her. "Are you mad at me?"

"*Nee*. I know I'm being silly. But Aden, I really, really don't want to go back to the pond."

After studying her face for a long moment, he motioned toward a dry patch of ground that had been shielded from the drifting snow by the tree's branches and sat down. "You don't have to. Let's just sit here for a few moments. Okay?"

Not completely trusting him, she shook her head. "I'd rather not."

"Please? Just for a minute or two? Until we catch our breath?"

Knowing that he would surely pull her down beside him if she didn't follow his lead, she sat. As soon as she did, he surprised her again by pulling her a little closer.

After a brief pause, he slipped not one but both of his arms around her, safely enclosing her against his warm, solid body. Surrounding her with his scent, with everything Aden.

For a time he didn't say a word, seeming to understand that she needed the time to quietly get herself under control. Little by little she relaxed against him, and as her breathing returned to normal, she became aware of how good it felt to be held by him.

Truly, it was the stuff of her dreams. But of course she'd never imagined the first time she'd feel his arms around her would be when she was having a panic attack at the edge of the frozen pond.

After another few minutes passed, he murmured, "Christy, one day we should go over there and skate. I know it will be hard, but I think your fears will ease if you face them. After all, you used to love to skate. You used to fly across the ice. Remember?"

"That's in the past."

"It doesn't have to be."

"That's easy for you to say."

"It's not. I hate seeing you so upset. I hate to see you cry. But I care enough about you to help you get through this."

She could hardly even stand on the banks! "I think not."

"I'll be with you. It will be all right. . . . I would never leave your side."

"Aden, it doesn't matter. I can't ice-skate ever again."

"When we get on the ice, I swear I won't let anything happen to you. You know that, right?"

"My fear, it's not slight. It's big, Aden. Massive. It consumes me." Staring hard at him, she ached for him to understand. "I've had it so long, I don't know if I'll ever get over it."

He lowered his head. They were so close, she literally had

to move her head back so their noses didn't brush each other. "You will, Christy. If you want to, you will."

"You sound so certain."

"I am. I believe in you."

She noticed his gaze drift over her face. And then, just like that, everything between them changed. No longer was she shaking because of fear; instead she was trembling because she was in his arms.

No longer was she thinking about her worst fears, but instead recalling her best fantasy.

Watching him, she noticed his gaze had turned heated. He glanced at her lips. Glanced again.

And right then, though she had little experience, she knew what was about to happen. Just as she knew if she pulled away he would let her.

When she met his gaze again, he was still staring at her. A fierce longing lit his eyes, turning the caramel shade to a darker brown.

She inhaled, mesmerized.

For a brief moment Aden looked as if he was debating with himself. Then, with a sigh, he shifted his arms, leaned close, and kissed her.

His lips brushed against hers gently. Once, twice.

She closed her eyes and sighed. And right then, right there, the very worst place on earth somehow became the very best.

Suddenly, she hoped they'd never ever leave.

chapter eleven

Having Christina in his arms was everything Aden had imagined it would be. She felt pliant and soft. Feminine and sweet. Innocent and trusting.

All the love and tenderness he'd felt for her for half his life bubbled to the surface and he ached to fold her back into his arms. Closer. And never let her go.

As he gazed into her lovely light blue eyes, he saw happiness shining in their depths, and he knew that happiness was surely a reflection of his own eyes. For too long he'd dreamed about this moment. And it was just as perfect as he'd always imagined it would be.

It was also the very thing he'd sworn to himself would never happen. Appalled, he pulled away from her and jumped to his feet.

Christina swayed as she regained her balance. "What in the world, Aden?"

He had to give it to her. Christina might be younger and innocent and have an irrational fear of a frozen pond, but one thing was for certain—she was no shrinking violet. While some girls might feel awkward and shy, she was looking at him with something akin to irritation.

And because he spied the same passion in her eyes that he was trying his best to keep at bay, he took another step back. And did the right thing.

"Christina, I'm so sorry."

She got to her feet, taking time to brush off the back of her dress. Only then did she look directly at him. "What exactly are you sorry for?"

How could she ask that? "You know what. For taking you here. For forcing you to stand on the bank." He took a breath and made himself say what he was really sorry about. "For kissing you."

Something flickered in her eyes. "You regret our kiss?"

No. "Yes."

"Because?"

He had no idea. "Ah, because you are so much younger."

"I'm barely two years younger, Aden."

"You were in a vulnerable situation."

Her eyes narrowed. "I was vulnerable. I was terrified of standing next to the skating pond."

"I know." That excuse would do as well as any.

To his dismay, she stared at him a good long moment. "And you think that I kiss men when I am afraid?"

Now he felt his cheeks burn. "Christina, you know that's not what I think." He felt as flustered as a teenage boy on his first date. And though this might have been her first kiss, it certainly wasn't his.

And because of that, because he felt more flustered than she seemed to be, he strove to regain some control of the situation. "You know what? I think it would be best if we didn't talk about that kiss any longer. We need to get back. I'm sure your parents are wondering where we are."

"I'm sure you are right." She turned and started walking toward the house, her steps even and sure.

And because he was a fool, he rushed to her side and then overtook her, wanting to lead the way. Because, well, he was the man. And because he had completely lost control of the situation. And because no matter what he said, he still wanted to be by her side.

Christina muttered something under her breath that he was glad he couldn't hear.

If he'd been alone, he would have hung his head. He was acting like a jerk. In so many ways.

Luckily, the house loomed just ahead of them.

Lucky, too, their time next to the pond had given them a little burst of energy. At least now he knew she wasn't exhausted and weepy.

When they were close enough to see that most of the family was outside watching for them, Aden attempted to interject a thread of joy in his voice. "Christina, would you look at that? We're almost back. And it looks as if Maisey alerted everyone that we were on our way, too."

"*Jah.* Isn't that something? It's *wunderbaar,*" she echoed. Sarcastically, for sure.

If they weren't so close to her family, he would have turned around to see her expression. Instead, he made do with giving her a little warning. "I don't think anyone needs to know what happened at the pond. We should probably keep what happened to ourselves."

"Aden? You don't want my parents to know that you wrapped your arms around me and that we kissed? Why on earth not?"

He slowed his pace, so that they were now walking side by side. "You know why," he bit out, not trusting himself to say anything else. Then he made things worse by taking her hand.

He told himself he was only taking her hand to keep her with him so that he could force her to listen. To see reason.

But that had obviously been an egregious error.

Because her eyes glittered with triumph. And then, to his dismay, her fingers gripped his securely, practically trapping his hand in hers.

Even though it was likely that her parents and siblings were going to see them holding hands.

"Obviously, I don't know much anymore, especially since you're a whole two years older than me. Why don't you explain things to me, Aden? Do you think my parents will imagine that there is something between us?" She looked pointedly at their linked hands. "Something special?"

There was something special, of course. There always had been. "You know, sarcasm doesn't become you."

Her chin rose. "Well, lying doesn't become you."

And then she had the audacity to smile when he attempted to pull his hand away.

"Oh, no, Aden," she whispered. "You reached out to me. You slipped your hand in mine. You're keeping it there a few seconds longer. And right at this moment, I hope my whole family sees us holding hands."

Now he was blushing. Blushing! "Christina—"

"Mamm! Daed!" she called out right over his words. Right over whatever he had been about to say to attempt to defuse the situation.

Not that all that much would have been possible. So far, he was doing a fairly good job of messing everything up. He'd become a master of saying the right words while doing the wrong thing.

"We made it back, safe and sound. It's so good to see all of you," she added as both of her parents walked toward them, dressed like Eskimos.

"Thank the good Lord," her mother said with a happy smile. "We were starting to worry!"

"You shouldn't have worried. After all, Aden was with me. And he would never let anything happen to me." Raising her eyebrows, she smiled sweetly at him. "Would you, Aden?"

When he pulled hard on his hand, she at last released her grip. Obviously happy to have it free, he gave his hand a little shake. And then stilled as he realized they were all awaiting a response. "That is true. I would never cause her harm."

Christina smiled grimly. "That is Aden, ain't so? He's so wonderful. Why, he's always thinking of me. Always thinking of what is best for me."

While he shot her a dark look, her mother clasped them both in her arms, one after the other. "When Maisey got here without you, my heart fairly leaped to my throat! I'll be having to say extra prayers tonight. Maybe even for the rest of the year."

"I'll be praising to Got, as well," her father said. "I started imagining that all kinds of terrible things happened to the two of you."

"I don't think we were in any danger. Were we, Aden?"

"Well, it was a long walk."

Her father clasped him on the shoulder as they started walking ahead. "What in the world happened?"

"No one had treated the roads. They got mighty slushy mighty fast. One minute Maisey was doing just fine, the next the buggy started sliding something awful. Christina and I elected to walk Maisey back instead of risk injuring her."

"When we got closer, Aden let her go on ahead," she explained. "He wanted to take a peek at the pond."

Aden felt his heart drop as both Joe and Martha stared at him in shock.

"We weren't there for very long," he muttered.

Christina smiled. "Just long enough."

Both of her parents stilled. "Long enough for what?" her mother asked.

"Long enough to stand on the bank," he said.

"Christina, I know that the pond can still bring up bad memories. That's a big step, you being able to get so close. And you did all right?" her father asked.

Aden inwardly groaned as Christina cast him yet another dry look. "Oh, sure. Aden stayed right by my side every step of the way. I am so grateful for his care."

"I would've felt terrible if something had happened to you," he said. "But you are fine, *jah?*" he asked. After all, if she was determined to talk in multiple meanings, he could, too. "No harm was done."

"I am perfectly fine. And you are right, Aden. I am no worse for wear after our little bit of excitement. Thank you again for seeing me home."

"You are welcome," he bit out. When her parents looked at him strangely, he pointed toward the barn. "I had best go take care of Maisey."

"You will do no such thing. The boys will take care of Maisey," her father said. "You two need to come inside and get warm before you get sick."

"I won't get sick, Mamm," Christina said.

"You might," her mother replied as she wrapped an arm around her daughter's shoulders. "One never knows what the Lord has in our future. All I do know is that even stranger things have happened. Ain't so?"

"You're exactly right, Mamm," Christina said. "Sometimes the strangest things happen when you least expect it. And pretending it never happened doesn't change a thing." Right before she entered the house, Christina glared at Aden over her mother's shoulder.

Feeling like his insides were twisted into a thousand knots, Aden felt more confused about himself and Christina than ever before.

The only thing he was certain about was that first thing in the morning, he was heading to the bank. The sooner he got out of Christina's life, the better it would be.

For both of them.

chapter twelve

"Jana, someone is here to see you," Marla called out in a sing-song voice from the doorway.

Glancing up from the computer screen in her office, Jana frowned. "Who is it?"

"That new policeman." Marla smiled. "The one who came down to the restaurant the day the Grabers' store got broken into. Remember him?"

Oh, yes she did. Ross Capshaw had been on her mind more than she cared to admit. It took everything she had to keep from smoothing out her dress and hair.

And though her interest was surely painfully transparent, she asked, "Did he actually ask to see me? Or, um, did he only come in for a meal?"

Marla looked delighted to replay the conversation. "Well, when I first sat him down, he asked if you were working today. Then, when I said yes, you were working, but that you were in your office doing paperwork and such, he asked if you usually came out to the dining room."

"He did?"

"Uh-huh." Looking especially amused, Marla said, "He looked real determined to see you, like it would make his day. So that makes me think that he came here looking for you, not just a bowl of soup. Don't you think?"

Yes, she did! Well, she hoped that's what it meant, anyway. "Maybe I should go see what he wants."

"I think that's a real good idea.."

Ignoring Marla's smirk, she said, "Well, then. I'll be right out." She certainly hoped that she sounded a whole lot cooler and blasé than she felt inside.

But Marla's amused grin told her that Jana wasn't fooling her for a minute. "Just to let you know, he ordered a glass of iced tea and then asked to look at the pie menu. I think that means he's intending to be here for a while."

"Um. Yes."

Marla winked. "I'll let him know that you'll be out shortly."

When she was alone again, Jana closed her door. Giving in to temptation, she fixed her makeup. And then decided she might as well pull a brush through her honey-gold hair.

And then she did what was most needed. She gave herself a stern talking-to. Just because he was the first man since Harrison she'd felt anything close to a spark with—it surely didn't mean that he felt anything like interest in her.

Why, he probably only stopped by to fill her in on the latest with the robbery investigation. And who knows? Maybe he was hoping to get another free piece of pie.

She'd probably imagined that they'd shared some kind of connection when they met. Why, who even knew what his status was, anyway? For all she knew, he had a longtime girlfriend.

And what did she care about all that, anyway? Wasn't she supposed to be done with dating at fifty-eight?

The moment she walked out of her office and into the kitchen, she scanned the room and saw both Ruth and Marla looking like they were trying very hard not to be interested in her business.

"You look real nice, Jana," Ruth said, obviously noticing her fresh lipstick and the way her hair was now neatly resting on her shoulders.

Jana debated whether to ignore the cheeky comment but then decided pride was way overrated. "Do you two think I look okay?" She frowned. "Or does it look like I'm trying too hard?"

"You look like yourself," Ruth said with a smile. "Real pretty."

She took a step toward the dining room, then gave in to temptation—and her small case of nervousness. "Marla, do you really think that policeman came back just for the pie?"

Marla's eyes twinkled. "Nope. When I went out to pour him tea, he asked if I'd talked to you. That has to mean something good. Don'tcha think, Ruth?"

Looking a bit like the Cheshire cat, Ruth nodded. "Most definitely."

Jana let herself smile. And gave in to temptation and revealed her thoughts. Marla and Ruth were her employees, but they were her friends, too.

And since Marla was married and Ruth widowed, she knew that they knew enough about life for her not to feel completely ridiculous about how giddy she was feeling. "It kind of feels that way to me, too. I mean, it's been a while since I've had a man show any interest in me, but it sounds promising."

"Mighty promising," Ruth said. "Now you'd best go on in that dining room before our newest policeman notices that the three of us are all standing here staring at him like a trio of bashful girls."

"Oh my gosh! That would be terrible!" With a shake of her shoulders, she gathered her courage, lifted her chin, and then strode out to the dining room.

There were a lot of people dining. Almost every table was filled.

But it didn't seem to matter. Right away, her gaze fastened on Ross. He was sipping a glass of iced tea and looking at something on his cell phone. Glad he was unaware of her—at least for the moment—she forced herself to scan the room.

It was gratifying to see more of the tables filled than usual. Pippa also looked to be handling the front counter with ease. They'd agreed to move forward with the partnership slowly. For now, Pippa was putting in a few hours a week working in different parts of the restaurant.

For a moment, she considered walking toward Pippa to see how she was doing. But when she met Pippa's eyes, the woman only winked.

Ah, it seemed as if everyone had noticed Ross's visit. Feeling like a child on a stage, she walked toward him. When she was just a few feet away, he stood up to greet her. Just as if they were on a date. "Hi."

"Hi," she replied. And then, because she was too old to try to even attempt to be coy, she added, "I'm so glad you came back."

"Me, too."

Just as she relaxed, a slow grin transformed his face. "Because, you know, the pie here is pretty wonderful."

"Ah. Yes, it is."

"But so is the company," he added with a smile. "Do you have time to join me for a little while?"

Even though she knew all the ladies were quietly watching them, she sat down across from Ross. "Do you have some news about the Grabers' store or the quilts?"

"Nope. We might get a lead, but I told Mr. Graber that he ought to look into a security system, or at least a couple of cameras. Sugarcreek is a wonderful town, but I'm afraid there's crime everywhere."

"Yes, I suppose so." She paused, wondering what else she could say about that topic.

After taking a sip of tea, he leaned back in his chair. "Would you mind if we didn't talk about robberies?" he asked quietly.

"What do you want to talk about?"

He shrugged almost boyishly. "Oh, I don't know. Maybe you."

"You really are single, aren't you?"

He laughed. "I promise, I really am divorced."

Why that gave her comfort, she didn't know. "How long ago did that happen?"

"Six years." He shrugged. "Candace is a nice woman. We just wanted different things. Maybe we got married too young?" He shrugged again. "Whatever the reason, we parted as amicably as two people who are divorcing can. I've been pretty much alone ever since. You?"

"Harrison died twelve years ago." She didn't see the need to admit that she'd been alone all that time. "So, are you seeing anyone?"

"I hope so." His eyes twinkled, making her feel sixteen again. She chuckled just as Marla came by.

"Want something to drink, Jana?"

"I'll take a glass of iced tea, too. And a slice of Ruth's buttermilk pie." Turning to Ross, she said, "It's good I don't mind running on the treadmill, because I eat way too much pie."

"I've never tried buttermilk pie."

"You should. It's my favorite."

Ross held up two fingers. "Two of those."

"I'll bring those out in a jiffy," Marla said. As soon as she turned, Jana heard a low chuckle.

And she started thinking that she didn't even care about that. This was the happiest she'd felt in just about forever.

Or at least in twelve years.

I won't be gone long, Judith," Ben said for about the tenth time as he slowly edged out of the living room toward the door. "At the most, two hours," he added. "Unless you'd like me to stay."

It took everything Judith had to keep a straight face. Her unflappable husband wore a look that was half helpless, half hopeful. She had a feeling that it would only take a frown on her part for him to cancel his plans and remain by her side.

But she was made of stronger stuff. And, besides, she was a little anxious to spend some time with James, just the two of them.

"Go on ahead, Ben. I have James in his crib next to me and a turkey sandwich and a bowl of potato soup that my mother fixed for me earlier today. I promise, I'll be fine."

To her amusement, he didn't budge. "I wish we had a phone. Do you think I should ask the bishop about getting a temporary phone?"

"Definitely not."

"But what if something goes wrong? What if you need anything—"

"I won't. Go."

He clasped the door handle at last. "All right. That is, if you're sure. . . ."

"Ben, what would my *mamm* say if I acted so helpless? She had a houseful and never let seven *kinner* upset her day in the slightest."

"She might have. Your *daed* might have done more than you think."

Even thinking about her father abandoning his duties at the store in order to fuss with a baby made her smile. She couldn't even imagine it. "Um, I don't think so." Knowing that if he waited much longer, Ben wouldn't leave, she made a shooing motion with her hands. "Off you go, now."

"All right. Good-bye."

When the door closed and she was finally alone with baby James, Judith grinned. "Now it is just you and me, James," she whispered.

Peeking into the crib, she was relieved to see he was still asleep. He'd been asleep only an hour. The last baby book she'd read said that a baby his age needed a good morning nap.

Satisfied that he was doing fine, she stretched out on the couch, yawned, and decided to spend the time until he woke up half dozing.

They'd survived their first night with the baby. He'd awoken twice, but between her and Ben, they'd managed to fix his bottle easily. He took it from her happily, burped, and almost instantly went back to sleep.

Thinking of Gretta's stories about her babies having gas and being confused about nights and days, Judith counted herself lucky. Of course, anything could happen. But so far, she privately thought she had taken to motherhood like a duck to water.

James squirmed a bit, threw his arms over his head, and then sighed and fell back into a peaceful slumber.

And she sighed in contentment. Amazing how these twenty-four hours had changed her life. Now she couldn't even remember why she'd been so taken aback with his color. So what if everyone in the world would know that she wasn't his birth mother? What mattered was that she was his mother in every way that counted. Years from now, she would tell James that very thing. That she'd prayed and prayed to God and He had rewarded her with the beautiful blessing of getting to care for James for the rest of her life. She felt like the luckiest woman in the world.

And if she ever let herself remember that she wasn't his adopted mother, merely a foster *mamm*? Well, she firmly pushed it aside. Surely the Lord wouldn't take him away from her.

She knew that she would do everything in her power to stop that.

This boy had her heart and she had no intention of ever giving him up. Not if she could help it.

chapter thirteen

The snow kept falling. Staring at it through her bedroom window, Christina wondered if she'd ever seen a more depressing sight.

A whole day had passed since they'd gotten back to the house. In that time, she'd taken a long hot shower, been wrapped into a thick flannel dress and slippers, and been ushered downstairs to have her fill of a giant bowl of chicken and dumplings.

None of her protests had been listened to or heeded. As far as her parents were concerned, she was a child again and clinging to the edge of death.

They'd asked her to stay home from work that morning, and because the snow was falling and she couldn't seem to do a single thing besides replay Aden's kiss in her mind, she'd agreed.

But now she wished that she'd gone in after all. Sitting around the house under her parents' watchful gaze was slowly driving her crazy.

She'd decided to spend the rest of the day working on an embroidery project she'd started three years ago. It was a sampler, and she was sure a careful seamstress could make the elegantly shaped letters and meaningful scripture verse into a thing of beauty.

All she seemed able to do was create more knots in the

floss. Thoroughly irritated with herself, she'd just pulled out her pair of embroidery scissors when Treva bounded into the room.

Christina stifled a sigh. She loved her sister, of course she did. But Treva had a determined way about her that reminded one of a sneaky cat. Treva liked to bait her sister with seemingly innocuous questions. Then, just when Christina would least expect it, she would pounce.

To make matters worse, Treva not only worked in a fabric store, she was practically a needlework prodigy. She could make anything that involved fabric, yarn, floss, or canvas beautiful.

"What are you working on?"

Christina sullenly held up the wrinkled mess of a sampler. "This."

When Treva winced, Christina glared right back at her. "I know. It looks awful."

Sitting next to her on the bed, Treva pulled the fabric from her hands like she was saving it from a terrible fate. Immediately, she began studying the stitches, even going so far as to run a finger along them. "These are all uneven."

"I know."

"And, um, some are even in the wrong spot. See this *D?*" she asked, pointing to it as if she was worried her sister couldn't even recognize the letter. "It's, um, backward."

Christina held up the scissors. " I know. I was about to repair it."

"Give me those."

Watching Treva painstakingly remove all of her work, Christina said, "Was there a reason you decided to bother me?"

"Yep."

"Care to tell me what it is?"

"You know."

"Actually, I don't."

Looking up, her sister smiled. "Two words. You and Aden."

"That would be three."

"Three?"

"Words," Christina sputtered, suddenly feeling more than a little off guard. But surely she was imagining things? After all, Treva had no idea about what, exactly, had happened between her and Aden last night.

Did she?

After staring at her a good long minute, Treva put down the offending fabric. "Mamm and Daed are in a bit of a state about what happened last night. But you know that, right?"

"It was hard not to notice. However, they need to calm down. We were late, but we weren't that late. And we had a good reason, too. We walked a long way in the cold."

Treva tilted her head and smiled slightly. "It's true that they were worried about you. But um, I think they have something more than your long walk in the dark on their minds."

"And what is that?"

"At the moment, they seem to be fixated on the fact that you were holding Aden's hand."

"Oh, for heaven's sake. It was nothing." She hoped her bluff sounded believable.

"Maybe not. But it was new."

"Did Aden overhear them?"

"Nope. After they force-fed him a second bowl of chicken and dumplings, and a huge slice of apple pie with vanilla ice cream, he escaped to the barn." She laughed. "Poor guy. He looked like he was about to burst."

"Mamm never does listen when we say that we've had enough."

Treva shrugged. "It's her way. We all know that. Now tell me what really happened between you and Aden."

Christina was tempted. She really was. But Treva couldn't always be counted on to keep a secret. And this was a pretty important one. "Nothing happened."

"If nothing happened, how did your hand become clasped in his?"

"Treva, don't be so silly. We were only walking together in the snow. I'm sure you've held Aden's hand a time or two."

"No, I don't think I have."

"Well, you saw how much it was snowing," Christina improvised, hoping this new tack would be more believable. "And I didn't have on good boots. Aden was merely making sure that I didn't fall."

"Oh." She sighed, a wistful, somewhat disappointed expression etched on her face. "That's too bad. I was really hoping it meant something else."

"What in the world could it have meant?"

"That the two of you have finally come to your senses."

Christina couldn't have been more shocked if, well, her whole family had been watching Aden kiss her. "Treva, what are you talking about?"

"Come now, Christina. Don't play dumb. You know as well as I do that Aden has always been fond of you."

"You think so?"

"We all know so!"

"I disagree. I mean, I would have noticed for sure."

"If you haven't noticed his regard, then you haven't been looking. Ever since we were all small, Aden has only had eyes for you."

"He cares about all of us."

"I think he does. But with you, he's different." Treva's lips curved up slightly. "He's a little more tender, a little more gentle. You're the first person he looks at when he sits down to supper—and usually the very last person he says good-bye to when he leaves the *haus*. He's smitten. He's *been* smitten for years."

"You're exaggerating."

"Maybe, but I doubt it." Waving a hand, Treva said, "I'm not sure why it bothers you. It's always seemed to me that the two of you were meant to be together." She lowered her voice. "Why, I'll never forget the way he acted, the way he looked, when he brought you home from the ice that day."

"That was a long time ago. . . ."

"It was ten years ago, but that doesn't mean I don't re-member it clear as day. Or that it didn't happen." Lowering her voice, her sister said, "He was devastated, Christina."

"I don't know what you want me to say to that."

"Oh, you. You've always been more closemouthed than the rest of us combined." She got to her feet. "If you're not going to share how you really feel, I'm going to leave you in peace."

"*Danke.*"

Looking even more irritated, Treva glared at her, then marched to the bed and snatched up the embroidery project, too. "I'm going to take this with me. You're going to com-pletely ruin it if you so much as touch it again."

"If you think taking that off my hands hurts my feelings, you're in for a big surprise."

"You, sister, are incorrigible," she said as she headed to the door. "I'm happy to take care of this for you. But let me tell you something. If you don't want Aden, that's your choice. But if you think you do, I suggest you actually do something about it. The sooner the better."

She truly didn't care for being bossed around by her little sister. "Or?"

"Or you're going to miss your chance, that's what. Nothing stays the same, Christina. Not even infatuation," her sister warned before opening the door and closing it not too lightly behind her.

Realizing she was once again sitting all alone—and no closer to figuring out what to do about Aden—Christina rested her forehead on the cold window and gazed out.

And started praying.

If it's Thursday, it means we've almost made it to the end of the week," Erik commented to Aden as they walked in one of the patients' rooms to retrieve a gurney and a portable medical cart.

"Almost," Aden replied with a smile, though he, for one, would have been happy for the week to continue forever. He was supposed to be off this weekend, and that meant he would have to spend even more time in the Kempf household.

Two days had now passed since he'd given in to temptation and kissed Christina in that snowstorm. But if the way things were at home were any indication, it might as well have been only a couple of hours. Everyone in the house—with the exception of himself and Christina—couldn't seem to stop talking about their long walk home.

Now to hear it, he and Christy had braved frigid temperatures, blizzard conditions, and a pack of roving wolves by the time they'd made it safely to the front door.

And that was nothing compared to the amount of speculation that revolved around the way he'd held Christina's hand.

No matter where he turned, yet another family member was wanting to know the real story about what had happened that night.

No matter how many times he stated that nothing had happened between them, all he got was a knowing wink or a sly smile from the boys, a glare from Treva, or increasingly irritated grunts from her parents. Even twelve-year-old Leanna had stated that she'd thought she could lie better than he did.

Smart people, those Kempfs.

After maneuvering the gurney out of the room, he guided it to the end of the hall and stripped it of all the sheets. He tossed them into the laundry bin, then made his way to the basement. Janice, one of the supervising nurses on his floor, had asked him to help inventory some new heart monitors. They were bulky instruments and required someone with a little muscle to maneuver them around.

So Janice had claimed.

"Hi, Aden," she said with a cheery smile when he entered the large storage room. "You're right on time."

"I try to be on time."

She laughed, the light, pretty noise making him smile. Janice was one year older than him and one of his favorite people to work with. She was easy to get along with and had a patient demeanor spiced with just enough salt and pepper to keep things interesting.

She was a Mennonite nurse and midwife by practice, but she was currently volunteering in a mentoring and training program at the hospital in hope of a raise.

It was because of this and the fact that he was the hospital's newest hire that they continued to be in each other's company so much. Apparently he needed a lot of mentoring.

"Now, what did you need me to inventory?"

With a frown, she pointed to a group of at least two dozen heart monitors. "These."

"What's wrong with counting these? It looks easy enough."

"Oh, it would be a simple job if the person who unpacked them did what he was supposed to and put all the cords and batteries with them like he was supposed to."

Now noticing a pile of forlorn-looking black rubber cords, Aden raised his brows. "It looks like these are our cords?"

"Yep." She held up an oversized plastic tub. "And these are our battery packs. Aden, we're going to need to open each monitor, find a matching cord and battery pack, and then make sure it all works together. Then charge the things."

She looked so irritated, he had to hide a smile. "If you show me what to do, I'll work on them by myself."

Her eyes widened. "But it could take you hours to inventory these all by yourself."

"That's fine. I know you'd rather be doing anything else than be stuck here in a back room checking instruments."

"That is true. This is the type of task that makes me want to pull my hair out. But aren't you supposed to get out of here in forty-five minutes?"

"I can stay late."

"You sure about that?"

"Positive. The van picks up until eight." Besides, the longer he was at work, the less time the Kempfs would have to interrogate him.

Janice stared at him for a long moment. Then, to his surprise, she bit her lip and looked almost shy. "It would be a shame to make you take a van home so late at night."

"Janice, I'm not one of your fresh-faced nurses," he joked. "I don't have a problem riding in a van in the dark."

"I wasn't worried."

"Good, because there was no need to be." He made a shooing motion with his hands. "Now, why don't you let me worry about these contraptions so you can go do one of the hundred things that's always on your to-do list?"

She laughed. "You know me pretty well."

"I know that you have a lot to do," he corrected, starting to feel a little bit awkward. He might have eyes for only Christina Kempf, but even he knew when a woman was gently flirting with him.

"You know, my shift ends at eight. Why don't you let me drive you home?"

Hmm. A new undercurrent floated between them that he wasn't quite sure what to do with.

But if he had a choice between taking a hired van and riding in Janice's car, there was no choice. "Janice, if you don't mind giving me a ride home, I'd surely appreciate that. It will be a nice change for me."

She smiled. "Great. I mean, that's great." She turned away, obviously ready to run to her next duty . . . then turned back around and met his gaze. "What about supper?"

"Excuse me?" This conversation was turning into a minefield.

"Are you hungry? Would you like to get something to eat on the way home?" She shrugged. "I mean, we've both got to eat."

He couldn't deny that. He was already hungry and he'd just volunteered to stay another three hours. And even though he was feeling a little awkward, he decided not to read anything into the offer. At the moment, it was simply dinner and a ride home from a coworker. "Supper sounds *gut*."

"I'm so glad you said that." Now her cheeks flushed and her eyes brightened. She looked younger. More feminine.

And he was realizing that there was nothing "simple" about what he was about to do at all.

"I'll meet you at the entrance to the staff parking lot in a couple of hours. Thanks, Aden."

"It's nothing. I mean, thank you." As he watched her walk away he knew it was time to stop lying to himself. In a few hours he was going to be leaving work with Janice and sharing supper with her. If it wasn't exactly a date, it was certainly close to being one.

And though he knew he wasn't all that sharp when it came to reading the female mind, he was enough of a man to understand what a blush and a shy smile meant. Janice was pleased about spending time with him.

Though a part of him wanted to scurry down the hall and tell Janice that he'd changed his mind, the rest of him recalled exactly how very good it had felt to hold Christina's hand. To hold her in his arms. To finally, after nearly ten years of longing and imagining and yearning, kiss her.

It had felt perfect. Exactly right.

And because of that? So very wrong.

No, it was a far better thing to concentrate on Janice. Besides, he'd already told Christina that he was seeing an English lady from the hospital.

Now he could hold his head up and be pleased that he hadn't lied. It was really too bad that it didn't give him even a moment of satisfaction.

chapter fourteen

As usual, Bernie showed up right on time.

As Judith stood in the doorway, watching the social worker park the car, then pull out her phone and affix it to her ear, she whispered into James's ear.

"We could set our day by Bernie's schedule, don'tcha think, James? She always shows up on time, listens to her messages, writes down a slew of notes, and then bounds out of her vehicle a scant five minutes later." Pointing to the car again, she said, "Look! Here she goes, writing down notes again."

James, of course, did nothing but stare up at Judith with his big brown eyes, melting her heart.

Unable to help herself, Judith bent her head and brushed yet another set of kisses on his forehead. He was adorable, and kissing and cuddling him was her new favorite pastime.

When his lips formed a soft oval and then broke into a happy smile, she felt as if she'd really done something special.

In the driveway, Bernie alighted from her car, her purse and an oversized tote bag resting on one of her arms. "You two look pretty as a picture," she called out with a smile.

"I feel like I should be in a picture," Judith replied. "Everything has been so perfect."

When Bernie got to the stoop, she reached out and brushed

a finger over James's soft cheek. "I'm guessing that means that the last two days have been going well?"

"Better than that. They've been *wunderbaar.*" Leading the way inside, she glanced over her shoulder. "Where would you like to sit?"

"I'm easy. I'll sit wherever you do."

"How about the kitchen? It's almost time for James to have his bottle."

"I'll follow you, then."

Only then did Judith realize that Bernie didn't seem to be acting quite like her regular self. Her smile wasn't as ready, her posture seemed a little stiff.

And she was still holding her tote as if her livelihood rested inside it. The last two times she'd visited she hadn't even brought it inside.

A thread of foreboding settled in. "Is something wrong?" Judith asked.

Bernie opened her mouth, shut it. Then held out her hands. "We do need to talk about something. Is Ben here?"

"No. He, um, went to our family's store to work for a few hours. Do you need him?"

"Not exactly."

"What does that mean? Is there a problem?"

"We'll talk about that in a few minutes. But first, how about I hold this sweet boy while you prepare his bottle?"

"All right. I mean, yes. Yes, of course." But when she handed James to Bernie she couldn't help but hold him a second longer than necessary. Almost as if she couldn't bear to part with him.

Almost as if she feared she wouldn't get him back.

Pushing that dark thought from her mind, Judith put the kettle on to heat water for the bottle and for the tea Bernie enjoyed so much. And then pulled out the plate of dried cherry and chocolate cookies she'd made early that morning.

"These look amazing," Bernie said, eying them with a look of true appreciation. "Cherry and chocolate?"

"*Jah*. They have oatmeal, too." She watched Bernie take an experimental bite, smile with pleasure, then go back to snuggling James while Judith bustled around the kitchen.

At last, she set a cup of hot tea in front of Bernie and had a bottle ready for James. "I'll take him now," she said, hardly able to contain her eagerness to have him back in her arms.

Luckily, Bernie handed him right over, seeming content to let Judith to feed James while she ate her cookie and sipped tea.

"What did you want to talk about?" Judith asked after another few minutes passed. She was starting to imagine the worst.

Bernie set her cup down and then crossed her legs with a small sigh. "I've been in contact with Kendra, James's mother."

"Oh?" She braced herself, dreading to hear that her worst fear was coming true. A small, terrible part of her feared that Kendra was about to be let out of prison. "Was she worried about James?"

"No. She is sad, of course, that someone else is looking after her baby, but she is truly delighted that he is with you." Bernie smiled. "She loves hearing about how much you obviously love her boy."

Judith did love him. Already, she loved him as much as if he were of her own flesh and blood. But of course she couldn't share such a thing. Bernie would think she'd gotten too attached to her foster child.

Choosing her words carefully, Judith murmured, "He is a *wonderful-gut boppli*. A true blessing."

Bernie reached for another cookie. "Indeed he is." She glanced at Judith, and then obviously seeing how nervous Judith was becoming, she put her treat down on a napkin and sighed. "Judith, there's no easy way to tell you this. Some of Kendra's relatives aren't real happy with James being raised out here in Amish country. They want him raised by family."

"What does that mean?" A sudden, horrible thought appeared. "Bernie, you aren't here to take him, are you? Are you taking James away from me?"

"No! No, not at all. But I did come over to tell you that it's Kendra's right to pursue this avenue. The courts like children to be cared for by family members if at all possible, instead of strangers."

Judith flinched. "But I'm not a stranger! Look." Even though she realized her voice had risen to almost a screech, even though she realized she wasn't making a lick of sense, Judith gestured to the baby, who was settled on her lap, happily nursing on a bottle.

She knew enough about babies from her sisters-in-law to know not all babes ate so well. "Look at him, Bernie. He's a happy baby. James is happy with me."

"I know he's happy. And I think you're doing a good job with him. But you are merely his foster mother." Bernie took a deep breath, visibly steeling herself. "Judith, if you will recall, I distinctly told you that fostering a child was not a first step to adoption." She regarded her carefully. "You told me you understood that."

"I did. I mean, I do."

"Then you must understand that my first priority has to be this baby's best interests."

"I do understand." But that was the crux of it, wasn't it? Judith realized. What made sense to the social worker, what made sense to the English laws, what even made sense to her brain didn't matter all that much to her heart. "But . . . can't you do something, Bernie? I'm not trying to take him away from his mother. I promise, I'm not. But she's in prison and he's happy here with me."

Bernie looked at her a good long moment, and reached for her bag. "Hold on a sec."

As the social worker dug in her tote, Judith felt her anxiety rise with each passing second. Of course, James felt her tension and pulled his mouth away from his bottle and began to squirm.

Tears filled her eyes. Judith attempted to blink them away before the other woman noticed. No way did she want Bernie to have a reason to take James out of her arms.

After opening up one of the folders, Bernie slipped on her glasses and skimmed the first couple of pages. Then she met Judith's worried frown.

"To be honest, I'm not all that sure how eager Kendra's relatives are to take on the raising of a baby. From what I understand, they all have their hands full with their own children and jobs. It says here that when my coworker talked to them she got the sense that they were offering for James out of a sense of obligation."

Just as Judith was about to blurt what she thought about that, Ben came in the back door.

The moment he saw her expression, his happy smile dimmed. "What's going on?"

"I had some news to share with you," Bernie replied, then proceeded to fill Ben in in her usual succinct way.

Just hearing about it all again made Judith feel even more frustrated.

As if he could read her mind, Ben rested a hand on her

shoulder for a long moment before taking a seat at the table, too. "So far, all you've told us is what these mysterious relatives want. What about James's mother? What does Kendra think? Has she stated a preference?"

"When we placed James with you, this was her preference. She told me that she hadn't had good relations with her two sisters for years. But, um, I guess that they've been talking to each other more. I think her sisters have visited her at the correctional facility a couple of times."

"So now they like each other?" Judith blurted.

Bernie paused, obviously choosing each word with care. "I think Kendra wants her little boy to be cared for by people who love him," she added diplomatically. "She wants him safe and happy."

"I do love him," Judith protested, not caring how attached she sounded anymore. "He is safe and happy."

Bernie's eyes softened. "I agree." After glancing at the paperwork in front of her, she added, "But that said, you cannot ignore the aunts' desire to see the baby."

"How would they see him?" Ben asked.

"Well, you have a couple of options. You can meet the relatives at a neutral spot. Or you could invite them here."

"Where do they live?" Ben asked. "Do they live far away? Would they even come all the way to Sugarcreek?"

"I don't know why they wouldn't. Unless you and Ben really don't want them at your house, I would recommend that they come here. That way little James would get to stay here, in comfortable surroundings. And it will give Kendra's two sisters the opportunity to see how James is living. They would get to see that everything is okay."

Judith felt her irritation grow. "Why wouldn't it be okay?"

"No offense, but sometimes when people hear 'Amish'

they think all kinds of crazy things. It's ignorance, of course. But if they visit you, and see what a nice home you have for the baby, well, I think, perhaps, that it will go a long way toward easing their minds."

Judith bit her lip and looked at her husband worriedly. "What do they think is happening?" After shifting James in her arms, she blurted, "I am so tired of folks imagining that I'm all that different from someone who drives a car."

Just as her husband placed a placating hand on her arm, Bernie smiled. "Now, don't get on your high horse, Judith. A lot of people have never been in an Amish home, have never met any Amish. Their only experience with the Plain people is from those creepy reality shows on television."

Judith wasn't sure what Bernie meant by that, but she did understand her point. It was always better to see things face-to-face instead of worrying about them. "Ben, what do you think?"

"I think we might as well let them come over. You'll be here, too, right?"

Bernie nodded. "Absolutely."

"Then I guess that's settled. Leave a message on the phone in the shanty about the date and time."

Bernie smiled as she closed the folder. "I wanted to talk to you about something else . . . something to consider."

"Yes?"

"You two might consider visiting Kendra at the prison."

Judith couldn't imagine such a trip. "Why?"

"It would be in your best interest to get to know the baby's mother, don't you think? Even if James never sees her again, he's going to be curious. And believe it or not, I think you'll find her to be on your side. Kendra has had a difficult life and made a lot of foolish choices. But she truly loves her son." Softly, Bernie added, "A mother's love for her child is a tangible thing. A wonderful bond. That's something we can't ever forget, right?"

Guilt edged into Judith's consciousness. She had been terribly selfish. Of course James's mother loved her baby. It was wrong of her to not want to remember that. "Of course."

"Judith and I are going to have to talk a bit about visiting Kendra," Ben said.

"Of course. I think that would be best."

Realizing that little James had fallen asleep, Judith stood up and carefully handed him to Ben, who deposited him in the crib she had in the sitting room.

Standing up, Bernie slipped off her glasses and placed her cup and saucer on the kitchen counter. "Thank you for the tea and cookies, Judith. As usual, you spoil me."

"Would you like some cookies to take home?" Judith knew Bernie lived on her own and often worked so late, she often made do with a couple of crackers or a frozen dinner when she got home at night.

"Not on your life! I'd eat them all in the car this afternoon. They were delicious, though." She paused. "So, you'll call me after you and Ben talk?"

"We will. Bernie, you've given us a lot to think about. And to talk about."

"I know this visit was difficult, Judith," Bernie said, her eyes full of sympathy. "If it's any consolation, I want you to know that I think you're doing a great job as a foster parent."

"*Danke*," Judith said, making sure she kept a pleasant expression on her face as she walked Bernie out.

After briefly hugging her good-bye, Judith stood at the door and watched the lady pull out her cell phone, grab her pen, and start writing notes again.

Then she walked back inside and thought about everything Bernie had suggested. It was going to be hard to visit James's family and go to a prison to meet his real mother.

But as she leaned back against the couch, she felt the Lord's presence. As strongly as if He were standing in the room with her.

"You knew I needed this, didn't you, Lord?" she whispered. "You needed me to stop being so selfish, to stop thinking only of myself and my needs. Instead, I need to remember that this isn't about me, it's about James. And that we do not live in a closet, hidden away from the rest of the world. He has family who loves him, just as I do. What is most important is remembering that Your will is what needs to be done."

She closed her eyes and gave thanks. And realized when she stood up again that she no longer felt a crushing weight on her shoulders. Instead, she felt lifted. Stronger.

Only the Lord knew who was the best person or people to take care of James. Only the Lord knew if James was destined to be Judith's child, or someone else's. And if she ever would have a baby to actually adopt.

But He knew best.

And as long as she remembered that, everything was going to be all right.

It might even be just fine.

chapter fifteen

Jana was staring at the message Ruth had taken and left on her desk when Pippa came into her office. "Pippa, Christina called in sick. We're going to be short a server again today."

Pippa's eyebrows rose. "Two days in a row? Does she do that often?"

"Never," she mused. "I guess she must really be feeling poorly."

"I'll go take her tables," Pippa said as she turned to leave.

"No. Wait a second. It's not too busy out there. Marla can handle everything. I wanted to see how you've liked working at the restaurant. You haven't said much."

Pippa smiled. "Well, I've been waiting to hear what you've thought about me being here. Do you think I'm fitting in? Do the other women seem okay with me being here?" She wrinkled her nose. "Or do you feel that they would rather not work for a girl like me?"

Pippa always came across as so confident, she must really be worried to be asking so many questions. "I've never seen you like this, Pippa. Has someone said something mean to you?"

"Not here. It's just that sometimes it's happened in the past. Once or twice."

Pippa's voice was thick with emotion. Jana's heart went out to her. "I am sorry to hear that. But as far as the Sugarcreek Inn goes, everyone loves having you here. The other girls have enjoyed getting to know you. I've been impressed with you, too."

Pippa's gaze warmed. "That makes me happy. If you think things are working out, I'd like to move forward. "

Actually drawing up the paperwork was a big step, but Jana knew it was time to move forward.

As Pippa stared at her, Jana thought about all the things she'd been missing out on. She could travel. She could visit her kids instead of hope they could find time to visit her in Sugarcreek.

She could even get to know Ross better. If she did that, she had a feeling that her life could definitely change. She would start living in the present and dreaming about the future instead of only recalling her past.

But only if she really made some changes.

At last, she gathered her courage and took the plunge. "Pippa, I would like our partnership to be seventy-thirty."

Pippa blinked. "I see. Well, um. I am not sure that I would want to run the inn with only a thirty percent ownership, Jana. I would feel like I didn't have any real authority, you see."

"Thirty for you?" Jana chuckled. "I'm sorry. Once again, I don't believe I explained myself. I meant you have seventy percent and I have thirty."

Pippa's expression changed from incredulousness to excitement to what could only be called fear. "Are you certain about that?"

"More certain than ever. Pippa, I not only want you to run the Sugarcreek Inn, I want you to feel like it is your restaurant now."

"And what are you going to do?"

"I, Pippa Reyes, am finally going to live."

At last Pippa smiled. That same wonderful, exuberant smile Jana had seen her wear when they'd first met and Pippa had first seen snow.

And that had to be her sign, Jana realized. Her sign that things were going the direction that God had intended. And that she intended, as well.

For the first time in a long time, Jana felt the fresh, warm, comfortable feeling of hope bloom inside her.

And it had never felt so good.

Pippa grinned. "Thank you, Jana. You won't regret this." They shook hands, and then the deal was made.

Privately, Jana thought nothing had ever felt as sweet.

The whole family surrounded Aden with a parade of questions after Janice dropped him back at the house.

At first he'd tried to brush off their curiosity—and his slight embarrassment about being observed being dropped off by an English lady—but he was fairly sure he wasn't succeeding.

No matter how much he tried to pretend otherwise, this was a new development, and it signaled yet another change and divide between him and Christina.

He was glad that he'd gotten up early and gone to the bank that morning. The banker was only too glad to discuss Aden renting the apartment above the vacant hardware store.

When Aden heard the price of the rent, he immediately asked when he could sign the papers. After that came another tour of the apartment, this time with an eye on repairs to make and what furniture he needed to buy.

Now, at the end of a very long day, he had the key to his

new home. All he had to do now was find the time to clean it up and make it his own.

But first he had to eat some ice cream with the Kempfs.

It was Leanna's birthday, and to celebrate Martha had bought everything for hot fudge sundaes.

After wishing Leanna a happy thirteenth birthday and making all the noises that were expected about having yet another teenager in the house, Aden sat down next to Christina.

So far she'd been doing a pretty good job of avoiding him. But he knew it was time to mend things. After all, he was now just days from moving out. "Ice cream sundaes taste good no matter what the weather, don't you think?"

"I suppose."

"Did Leanna have a good supper?"

"Oh, *jah*. We had fried chicken and french fries. Her favorite supper."

"That's my favorite, too. I'm sorry I missed it."

"Well, you had your own plans, didn't you?"

Ouch! "I told you that I had to work late. And that Janice had been kind enough to offer me a ride home."

"And go out to supper with you. We can't forget that," she said archly.

His ice cream dish was empty now, but Christina's was hardly touched. Thinking it might be best to push the focus off of himself, he said, "I hope you didn't have any trouble getting a ride home from the restaurant today."

"Actually, I didn't go into work today."

"You didn't? Was something wrong?"

"Not at all. I was just tired. And Treva reminded me that I never take any time off." She shrugged her shoulders. "I figured that maybe I was due for a break."

He didn't know what to say to that. "What did you do all day?"

She shrugged in an offhand way. "Nothing too special. A little of this and that."

"Such as?"

"I helped Mamm with a couple of chores around the house. Wrapped Leanna's presents. Oh, I embroidered, too."

"What? You hate embroidery."

"Not necessarily. I didn't hate it today."

He decided not to touch that one. He'd seen lots of her half-finished projects over the years. In his opinion, all needles needed to stay far away from her. "I'm glad you had a good day. I don't work tomorrow. Do you?"

She nodded.

After waiting a moment, he asked, "Do you need a ride either way? Or both ways? I'll be happy to take you."

"I'd hate to bother you."

"It's no bother. I'm going to be near the Sugarcreek Inn anyway."

"And why is that?"

"I'm going to look at an apartment tomorrow. Maybe even sign my lease." He decided it would probably be best not to tell everyone that the lease was signed and the key was in his pocket.

"Do Mamm and Daed know that you are doing that?"

"Does it matter? All of you know that I had planned to move out."

"Yes. You did tell us, didn't you? Since you've got a busy job. And an English woman friend."

Her sarcastic, clipped tone didn't sit too well with him. Neither did the fact that the way she said "English woman friend" could have been substituted with "dangerous ax murderer."

But as Aden watched her stand up in a huff, rinse out her dish, and then walk out of the room, he knew he was at a loss as to how to make things easier between them. The fact of the matter was that things needed to change between the two of them.

He couldn't go around holding her and kissing her anymore. If he stayed, he was liable to do it again.

Leaving had definitely become less a matter of choice and more a matter of necessity.

And given the way Christina was acting, it would be best for both of them if he left as soon as he could.

chapter sixteen

"That man came back," Marla said. "And I do believe that he's looking for you."

Christina looked up from the stack of napkins she'd been folding. "What man?"

"You know. That handsome man with the green eyes. The one you chatted with the other morning when he came in with his family."

"Oh, him? He said he was going to come in one day soon. But I've yet to see him make an appearance."

Marla shrugged. "Ain't no reason for you to get in a tiff about it. You know that life happens. Maybe he got called to work or something."

"Maybe. In any case, I'm not interested in him anymore." Without a doubt, she knew she wasn't going to be interested in any other man besides Aden Reese now that he'd kissed her. When she'd allowed his kiss, she'd known that she'd taken him into her heart.

And though he was currently full of regrets and infatuated with some fancy hospital nurse, she wasn't in any hurry to look around at another man.

Marla rolled her eyes. "Christina, sometimes I am certain that you are as stubborn as Miriam! Go on out there and at least be pleasant. It doesn't hurt anything to go out there and say hello. It might even help your case of the blues."

"Fine."

"*Gut.*" She made a shooing motion with her hands. "Now, off you go. Go smile and say hello. I chatted with him for a moment when I seated him. He's a farmer, living over in Walnut Creek."

Trying to become enthused, she said, "That's close."

"It is. He's also as handsome a man as I've seen in a long time. And he's friendly enough."

Christina looked down at the pale green skirts of her dress, neatly surrounded by the white apron all of them wore at the restaurant. She didn't want to go out to see him. Actually, ever since she'd had that fateful walk with Aden, she didn't want to do anything but moon over him and try to find a way to get him to see her as a grown woman.

But of course, he had moved on. He wanted her to know that, too. Otherwise he wouldn't have let that English nurse bring him home. Otherwise he would have deflected all their questions and told them directly that Janice meant nothing to him. That she'd merely given him a ride home. That was all.

But of course, he hadn't done that. Instead, he'd acted mysteriously, as if there was more to his story than he was willing for the whole family to know.

Further compounding the problem was his new apartment in town. Obviously, he was determined to put as much space between him and her as possible. As quickly as possible.

She could pretend that she either didn't notice or realize that there was no future between the two of them.

Marla crossed her arms over her chest. "Earth to Christina. Are you going to go see him or not? If you don't take his table, I'll need to. Or someone else will. We can't let him sit there by himself much longer. What do you want to do?"

Suddenly, it felt as if it wasn't about tables and orders.

It was about opportunities versus disappointments. It was about looking toward a future or remaining with her heart firmly ensconced in the past.

"I'm going out right now," she said, and then started walking forward before she let herself change her mind again.

Behind her, Marla chuckled. "Good for you, dear. We were hoping you would do that."

Marla's gentle push forward made Christina push her shoulders back and even manage to smile at the farmer. Who, she was delighted to see, had been eying the kitchen door with a watchful expression.

"You decided to return after all," Christina said when she reached his table. "Was the coffee irresistible?"

"It wasn't the coffee that brought me back."

His gaze was so direct, his unusual green eyes so filled with admiration, Christina felt her cheeks flush.

His gaze also gave her the courage to attempt to flirt a little. "Whatever the reason, I am glad you returned. Now, what may I serve you? Would you care for another piece of pie?"

He drummed his fingers on the table. "When do you get off?"

"Pardon?"

"When you get off, I was hoping that maybe we could go for a walk or something."

"I work until two o'clock today."

"That's not too far off. If I come back at two, would you take a turn with me around Sugarcreek?"

He was eager. It was exciting and nerve-racking, too. "I don't even know your name."

"It's Christy."

"Christy? That's a girl's name." Realizing what she'd said,

she clapped a hand over her mouth. "Forgive me. I'm not usually so rude."

But instead of looking offended, Christy laughed. "No worries. Believe me, I get that all the time. My real name is Christopher. Christopher Fisher. But I was named after an uncle, and I have a cousin Christopher, too. You know how that goes. Soon everyone was calling us Christopher One and Blond Christopher."

She giggled. "It always happens."

The farmer smiled. "After a while, Christy it became. It stuck. And I'm right fond of it, if you want to know the truth."

"I like it," she said politely. Though she had a feeling she'd never actually think of him as a Christy—that was Aden's pet name for her, after all—she did suppose that there was no harm in striking up a friendship with him. He was so very handsome. Striking, with perfect green eyes, brown hair the color of a mink in the winter, a square jaw. Somehow, it seemed to make sense that such an attractive man would have such a pretty name. It would be strange if he was a Frank or an Eli.

"So, what do you want to do? Are you going to let me take you walking?"

"I don't know. . . ." If she said yes she'd feel like she was betraying Aden.

"Come on. All I'm askin' is to spend some time with you when you're not working. Surely you don't think any harm can come to you by going walking with me down Main Street in the middle of the day?" Humor laced his voice and lit his eyes.

She looked away, embarrassed. She suddenly felt too young, too sheltered. Too timid.

"What do you say!"

It was time to make a decision. She could either continue to pine for Aden and wish things were different between the two of them. Or she could finally move forward and take a chance.

And put that way, there really was no choice.

"I would like to take a walk with you, Christy."

His lips curved into a genuine smile. "Are you ever going to tell me your name?"

"Oh, I'm sorry. Christina."

His eyes widened. "Now I understand why you looked at my name so strangely! Look at us—Christy and Christina. Now, there's a pair."

She laughed. It felt so good to laugh and tease another boy. Felt so good to stop worrying about a hundred past experiences, hoping each one could be overlooked and/or forgotten. "*Jah*," she murmured, happy with herself for taking a chance. Happy to be chatting with someone who she didn't share years and years of memories.

Who didn't make her pulse jump just by walking into the room. "We are quite a pair," she replied at last. "For sure and for certain."

chapter seventeen

Jana was blessed with four absolutely wonderful kids. Each was unique, and each had been supportive of the business and of her schedule over the years. When they were younger, they'd even each had a turn working at the restaurant.

When they finished high school, each had gone off to college. Slowly but surely, their length of time at home had gotten shorter and shorter. Now Nick was married with two children, Melissa worked in Cleveland, and Jane was all the way out in San Francisco. The three of them were now so busy with their lives, it seemed even their phone calls were rushed.

Only Garrett, her youngest, seemed at loose ends. But that didn't mean he stopped by to see her or call her on a regular basis.

She didn't expect him to. Kids were supposed to grow up and be independent. Although she'd had her own growing pains about them all leaving the nest, she'd managed to muddle through. She'd sold the house, worked hard at the restaurant.

And now she was even taking time for herself, working with Pippa and easing into a comfortable partnership with her. Thinking about how Ruth and Marla got along with Pippa so well, Jana realized that she'd been a fool to wait so long to step away. The Sugarcreek Inn was not only doing just fine under Pippa's leadership, word had spread that the restaurant was trying out some new dishes. Each day it seemed that more tables were filled.

Obviously, change was a good thing.

So was her new relationship with Ross. After three visits to the restaurant, Ross had admitted that he couldn't eat another piece of pie . . . but that he'd love to take her out to dinner someplace else.

She was surprised by how good all the change felt in her soul.

Which was probably why she was feeling so stung by Nick's current strand of conversation.

Juggling the phone to her ear, she cleared her throat. "Nick, you are sounding a bit judgmental. Son."

"I'm not being judgmental; I'm just saying that lately it's been really hard to get a hold of you."

Smoothing back her hair, she put on her reading glasses and sorted through the mail while she shifted the phone under her chin yet again. Perhaps if she focused on bills she wouldn't feel so frustrated.

"Restaurants don't run themselves, dear. You don't need me to tell you that. If someone doesn't show up or there's a problem, I have to be there. This is nothing new."

"Mom, I know what's in your bank account. You don't have to work another day in your life if you don't want to."

"Your father did leave me financially secure. . . ."

"It's not just what Dad did. You've done a great job with the restaurant, and you made some good investments, too. I hope I do as well with my finances as you've done with yours."

"Thank you for the compliment."

But of course, what she was really wondering was why he was bringing up her financial situation.

"So why aren't you enjoying yourself more?"

The question caught her off guard. She'd been meaning to tell the kids about Ross, but so far she hadn't gotten the nerve to do it.

They'd had a hard enough time with her selling their childhood home—she had no idea how they'd react to her dating Ross. He was as different from their father as night and day. Their father had been bookish and a bit of an introvert.

Ross wasn't exactly gregarious, but he was a doer. He liked to go walking, hiking. Biking. He liked to talk to people. He liked to talk to her.

"Mom, you hardly come over to see Dylan," Nick continued. "And Melissa and Garrett said you haven't seen them in weeks."

He'd called his siblings? "That isn't all my fault. You've been too busy to come see me. When I talked to Melissa the other day, she was almost too busy to talk on the phone."

"Have you called Jay lately? She's dating someone. Finally."

Jay, just one year older than Garrett, had actually been named Jaynilyn. Her little tomboy had famously claimed she'd rather be called plain old Jay when she was five years old. Harrison had thought that was the funniest thing he'd ever heard and had immediately started calling her Jay.

In addition to being a tomboy, their Jay had also been famously single-minded. Instead of dating she'd studied. Instead of thinking about relationships, she'd thought about her next promotion. Now she was living out in California, working in San Francisco in the corporate offices of a fancy gift and jewelry store.

But Jana sure hadn't heard a thing about her being in a relationship. "Jay told you she was dating?"

"Well, she told Melissa, who told Garrett, who told me."

Jana swallowed hard. Her four children had been calling one another. A lot. But though they had time for that, they had elected Nick to give her this call.

Stacking some old magazines in a pile to take to the recycling bin, Jana struggled to keep her voice soft and easygoing. "My goodness. Jay hasn't told me about that. Yet."

"Maybe she didn't tell you because you haven't been answering the phone."

"I've had my cell phone, Nick. I promise, I would have heard if it rang."

"Jay said she called you on Saturday night."

Which was when Ross had taken her to the movies. "Hmm."

"Hmm? Mom, I'm not trying to make you feel guilty. I'm just pointing out that you're putting the restaurant in front of people who care about you."

"You're doing pretty good at the guilt. . . ."

"Mom, this isn't about me or the other kids."

"What is it about then?" Her voice had turned tart. She hated that, but she was feeling guilty and a bit frustrated, too.

"You."

"Me?"

"Mom, when was the last time you took a vacation, or did something just for you?" He paused, then added, "When was the last time you went on a date of your own, Mom?"

Well, here was her chance. "Actually, I . . . I have been dating someone."

For a good ten seconds, there was silence. "You have?" To say his voice was incredulous was an understatement.

"Yes. It's only happened recently." She paused, then shrugged her shoulders. "On Saturday night, I didn't hear my cell phone because I was at the movies with Ross."

"His name is Ross?"

She couldn't help notice that Nick skimmed right over the point of her statement—that she hadn't been at work, she'd been at the movies. "Yes, his name is Ross. And before you ask, he's a nice man. He's a police officer right here in Sugarcreek. Isn't that something?" she mused, maybe a little too offhandedly. "I never thought I'd date a policeman."

"Who have you told about this?"

"Well, the girls at the restaurant know."

"But none of us? Why haven't you told any of us?"

"Nick, I thought I'd wait a bit. You know . . . see where things went." She bit the inside of her cheek since she could only imagine how her oldest, type-A son was handling the news.

"Mom, maybe I should come over to see you soon."

She smiled. She bet he wanted to come out! "I would love to see you. And Kara and Dylan, of course. You know how much I'd love that."

"I was thinking, maybe I could help you come up with a business plan, you know, a timeline so you could start thinking about selling the restaurant."

"Dear, I actually already have a plan. There's the cutest new girl in town who was interested in eventually taking over the place. Her name is Pippa. We've already begun the paperwork to become partners. Actually, it's working out really well."

"You did that without asking me? Wow."

He sounded hurt. And she felt bad about that. But not that bad. It was her restaurant, not his. "It just kind of happened, Nick. Kind of like Ross."

"Mom, you know what? I think it would be great if all of us came out to Sugarcreek to see you."

All four of them now! "I would like that very much," she said as casually as possible. Thank goodness he couldn't see her look of amusement. "Perhaps we could plan something at Christmas."

"No, I think I'll see if we can do something a lot sooner than that."

"Nick, if you're worried about me or my decisions, I'll have you know that I do not appreciate you second-guessing me."

"I'm not second-guessing, Mom. But I am going to go ahead and call Garrett, Jay, and Melissa as soon as we get off the phone."

"You sound a little panicked, dear. I promise, I'm fine."

"When I talk to everybody, we'll discuss everyone's schedule. Then I'll call you back when we come up with a date."

He sounded very sure that he was going to be able to convince them all to drop what they were doing and to zip out her way very soon. Obviously, her eldest was extremely concerned that his usual stuck-in-the-mud mother had started actually doing something with her life.

But instead of arguing, she gave in gracefully. After all, she did want to see all the kids, and it was probably a good idea for them to meet Ross sooner rather than later.

"All right," she said in a breezy way that probably didn't fool her son for a second. "Just let me know when all of you would like to come out this way. You know how much I love to see you."

"Okay, I'm going to call everyone. I'll call again soon. Love you."

"All right, dear." She smiled broadly. "Talk to you soon."

When she hung up, she found herself both bemused and more than a little bit amused.

It seemed that the best way to connect with four grown

children was actually not to call them often or complain about not seeing them enough.

And in her case?

All she'd had to do was move on with her life.

It only took fifteen minutes for Aden to wish he'd never taken Martha with him to visit his new apartment.

Martha Kempf was a generous and very kind woman. But she also was not happy about him moving out into a run-down apartment above an empty hardware store. From the moment she walked through the door with its three locks, her posture changed.

And then her expression did, too.

All the while, it was obvious she was trying her best to keep her opinions about his new home to herself. And that, Aden feared, made the tour all the worse.

"How much did you say the rent was again?"

Though she'd already asked him three times, he repeated the amount.

"And that is per month, you say?"

"*Jah*, Martha, that is right. And we also know you heard it correctly the first time, too."

If she was ashamed that he caught on to her game so quickly, she didn't show it. Instead, she lifted her chin a little, attempting to look down at him from her diminutive height of five-foot-two. "All I'm saying is that it seems mighty expensive for a place such as this."

"I think you're forgetting that it's a pretty good size." He waved a hand around the place, just like he'd suddenly become a real estate agent. "It's got this generous living room, a bedroom big enough for a king-sized bed, and lots of closets, too."

"*Jah*, this is true. But it doesn't have much else."

Aden decided to refrain from asking what else Martha thought it needed.

Taking a turn around the place—yet again—she wrinkled her nose at the stain on the floor in the living room. "It is also in need of a real good cleanin'."

"It hasn't been lived in for a few months." Not since Miriam's friend Mary Kate had gotten attacked by her exboyfriend, he knew. Of course, he wasn't going to share that one. He sincerely hoped Martha wouldn't make that connection anytime soon.

"The bedroom is rather dark, don't you think?"

With a tug, he pulled the shade up "It looks better now. Like I said, it's a good size."

"Perhaps." She shrugged, obviously not ready to give an inch. "Aden, I am sorry, but I fail to see how this place is an improvement over your current situation. You have a nice bedroom at our *haus*. And it is on the side of the house, away from the *kinner*. You've got some space to yourself, too."

But that was the point. He didn't have enough privacy. And he certainly needed more than a couple of hallways separating him and Christina. "It is time, Martha. We both knew that I couldn't live with you forever."

"I agree with you, to be sure. But I never imagined you would be in such a hurry. And especially not to go to a place such as this."

Her voice was more than a bit critical. One of her fingers was held up like a trophy, the dust decorating it seeming to be a symbol representing everything that was wrong with the tiny place above an abandoned hardware store.

It occurred to him that he should be a little bit offended.

After all, Martha could have at least pretended to find something good about his new home.

But Aden was just trying to get through this. "It is simply time for me to move. Everyone grows up, you know. And this place has promise."

"Hmph. That's about all it has." With a bit of a dramatic sigh, she led the way toward the kitchen, perhaps better described as a tiny kitchenette. "This isna much. You'll barely be able to boil water here.'

"I think you're exaggerating a bit." He waited a moment, then looked her square in the eye. "Maybe a little bit more than that. What is wrong, Martha?"

"I'm not ready for you to move away. I didn't think we'd have to go through this until you were getting married. And then it would be to a real house. Not a dreary place like this."

"Not everyone gets married young. I needed to move out on my own." Reaching out, he squeezed her hand. That soft hand with the faint smattering of freckles across the knuckles. Keeping her hand in his for a little longer, he looked at how their hands looked together. He'd always thought his adoptive mother had pretty hands. They were capable and strong, but also had the pale skin of the rest of the family. He'd always imagined Martha as a time machine, giving him a glimpse of how Christina would look in twenty years' time.

Which made him realize how he would always think that Christina was the prettiest girl in the world.

"Please try to be at least a little happy for me. It would make it easier for me."

A new awareness settled into her eyes. "There's more going on than I realized. Does it have to do with the nurse who took you home?"

"Janice and I are merely friends."

"But maybe you're hoping for something more?" She raised a brow. It was obvious that she was feeling pleased with herself, thinking that she'd solved the mystery of why he'd decided to move out.

"I didn't say that."

She tapped her temple like she'd just solved a case. "You didn't have to, Aden."

He didn't like her thinking he was interested in courting an English nurse. But he supposed it was better for her to think that he liked Janice than to go back to dwelling on the way he'd held Christina's hand.

Now that he'd gotten a taste of what it felt like to be in the middle of everyone's speculating, he decided that there was no way he going to admit his real reason for leaving. But he was tired of saying the same thing, so he kept silent.

After another long look, Martha nodded at last. "Joe and I will gather everyone and help you move. Just tell us the date and we'll help you."

"There's no need to go to so much trouble. I don't have much, anyway."

Martha raised her brows. "You have enough. Definitely too much for one person to try to carry up those rickety steps."

He wasn't quite sure what she was talking about, since he'd come to the Kempf house with nothing but his clothes and a few personal items. "I can manage a couple of duffel bags of clothes, Martha."

"You have much more than that, Aden! You have your bed and dresser. You have the kitchen table that's up in storage in the barn." Finally warming up to the topic, she added, "I'll look around some other places, too. I seem to remember that we might have a pair of chairs in the basement that I've been anxious to replace."

"I can't take those things."

"Why on earth not?"

"They're yours, not mine."

"We're giving them to you, Aden."

"But don't you think they should go to your own *kinner* instead of me?"

Looking over him carefully, her usually melodic voice turned snippy. "Well, my goodness. I must say I'm mighty disappointed in you, Aden Reese."

"Why?"

Still frowning and looking put-upon, she continued. "After everything I've done for you, I never thought I'd hear you talk like this." She waved a hand in front of her chest. Practically acting like she was about to have a heart attack.

"I think you're being a little dramatic there, Martha."

"Not hardly. Here for ten years, Joe and I have done everything we could think of to make sure you knew you were an important part of this family."

"I know you have—"

Her voice turned a little more strained. A little more plaintive. "Why, we gave you that bed when you came to us. You always said you slept *gut* on it."

"I did. I mean, I have."

"Then you must understand that there's no way I would ever let you continue on your way without it." She waved a hand in the direction of the dark bedroom's doorway. "If you are going to insist on sleeping in this place, I certainly am not going to let you sleep on the floor."

"I wasn't going to sleep on the floor. I was going to go to Millers and order a bed."

"You were going to buy one? I think not."

"All right, Martha. I hear you. *Danke*."

"And you will accept the other things, too."

"You're not worried that Nate or Henry will want those things?"

"*Nee*. I am not. Don't make me argue with you, Aden."

"I don't want to argue with you, either."

"*Gut*." Looking a bit mollified now that she'd gotten her way, Martha clasped her hands together. "Now, all this brings us to another thing. All of us girls will come over here tomorrow and help you clean."

Not only would he feel horrible about bringing them extra work, there was something about the thought of Christina washing out his shower or kitchen sink that gave him the willies. "That is not necessary."

She sighed dramatically. "Aden, must we go through this all over again?"

Looking into her eyes, he realized that his adoptive mother was determined to get her way. "Of course not. I will be thankful for your help."

"*Gut*. That's more like it. Now, walk me down the stairs. I never thought I'd say this, but I just don't think I'm brave enough to go down those narrow, rickety stairs by myself."

"Of course. I had intended to help you." As he took her arm, he guided her down the steep and rickety wooden steps. His new landlord had promised that the steps would be repaired shortly. But in the meantime they were one step away from being blown down by a fierce wind.

After they got downstairs, they walked down the narrow alley that led to Main Street. "What are you doing now?"

"I'm going to head over to the Grabers' store. I saw Joshua Graber at church and he told me they got a new shipment of fabric in last week. I thought I'd take a look at it while I wait for Christina to get done with her walk."

"Walk? You mean *work*, right?"

"*Nee*, I mean *walk*. Christina was asked to take a walk after work."

"It's freezing outside. Who would want to do that?"

"A man who wants to go courting, I imagine," she retorted.

"Wait a minute. She's being courted?"

"Well, now, I don't know if that is quite what is happening. She met a man at work, you see. Today he asked her to take a walk with him. When I stopped over to see her while you were in the bank she told me about it."

"He's a stranger and you're letting her spend time with him?"

"It's not like I have a lot of choice. You know Christina. She's a woman who knows her mind."

"But she doesn't always make the best decisions."

"No, she seems to have a pretty level head." She looked at him curiously. "Aden, why are you so upset about this? There's nothing wrong with going for a little walk in the afternoon. And Christina is of age. It had to happen sooner or later."

"I'm not upset. Just concerned." Aden knew he was acting a bit proprietary. The right thing to do was to not say another word about this. As it was, he was making his adoptive mother very amused. And he was sure that looking back on things in a few hours he was going to be embarrassed about his runaway mouth. But some things couldn't be helped.

"It's sweet of you to be so concerned, but I think you're worrying over nothing. Christina said they spoke a time or two at the restaurant."

If he was a regular at the restaurant he had to be local. "Who is it? Do you know him? What is his name?"

"He's no one I know. Believe it or not, he goes by the name of Christy."

"Christy?" He relaxed a bit. Obviously, Martha had things a little mixed up. Most likely Christina was going for a little stroll or shopping trip with one of her girlfriends. "Martha, I'm thinking you got a little confused. Christy is definitely a girl's name."

"To be sure it is. But in this case, Christy is short for Christopher. He told Christina that he was named after an uncle, and that he had a cousin with the same name."

"I think that's odd."

She shrugged. "I had a cousin that we all called 'Red Jim' because he had red hair. You know how these things go." Scratching her head, she mused, "Come to think of it, I think Joe had a similar situation with some of his cousins."

Aden was hardly paying any attention to Martha's chatter. He was still trying to get his head around the fact that Christina was going to be spending time with another man. "Well, it just seems a bit rash, letting Christina be alone in the company of a boy no one knows."

"I don't think he's a boy, dear. Christina said he looked to be just a year or two older. But I'm sure we'll hear more about it later. I mean, I will. When I pick her up in an hour."

She sounded a little aggrieved by the thought of waiting . . . which was all the opening he needed. "You know, there's no reason for you to hang around town all this time. I'll be happy to wait for her."

"Aden, there's no need. You are a busy man. I'm sure you've got a dozen things planned to take care of in order for you to move into your apartment here."

"I'll be able to get a lot of things done while I wait for Christina."

When she looked as if she was about to argue some more, he wrapped an arm around her shoulders. "Please let me do this. I like watching out for her."

Her expression softened as she leaned into his brief hug. "I know you do, Aden. And just between you and me? I do believe she likes you looking out for her." With a little shake of her head, she added, "I honestly don't know what Christina is going to do when you leave us. Sometimes, I fear it's going to break her heart."

The lump in his throat had returned. "We'll see you in a few hours."

"Be careful in the weather." She scurried down the street before he could say another word, which he was thankful for.

Christy was nice. He was friendly and had a lot of information about all sorts of topics. So far, in the fifteen minutes that they'd spent together, he'd told Christina about his produce company, the proper way to fertilize roses, and how destructive deer and rabbits can be.

She'd agreed with him on all sorts of things, mainly as a way to keep him talking.

Because she'd learned after five minutes that Christy Fisher was nothing like Aden Reese. It seemed finding the right man—correction, make that another right man besides Aden—was going to be a bit more difficult than she'd imagined it would be.

Now, as they traipsed up and down Main Street, bundled up against the westerly wind that Christy said was full of the smell of new snow, avoiding shoppers and brown and gray piles of old snow that littered the sides of the sidewalk,

Christina wondered how much longer it would be until they'd walked a full hour.

"Now, I've tried a variety of organic fertilizers, though nothing works quite as well as chicken droppings on my prize rosebushes," Christy intoned.

She winced. She knew enough about chickens to not be enamored of anything about them. She'd also cleaned enough coops to prefer not to hear anything about chicken poop and roses.

Feeling more weary by the minute, she glanced toward the Grabers' store. Her mother was over there looking at fabric. Though it might be a bit rude, Christina decided it was time to tell a white lie and cut things short. "I'm so sorry, but I'm afraid it's time for me to go."

"Why?"

"Well, my *mamm* is over at the Grabers'. I don't want to keep her waiting. Especially if there's snow coming, you know."

Christy looked up at the sky. "When I said snow was on the way, I didn't mean right this minute." He frowned. "Let's walk a little farther. I want to spend more time together."

"That's mighty sweet of you to say."

"I'm not being sweet. I mean it. I want to get to know you better. Here I've been talking so much, I've hardly learned anything about you."

"Um. Well . . ."

"Christina? There you are."

She stilled. And almost smiled. She would know that voice anywhere. Turning, she saw Aden walking toward them with a forest-green wool scarf wrapped around his black coat's collar.

"Hi, Aden. I didn't know you were in town today."

"I needed to look at my new apartment." He smiled. "Actually Martha wanted to see it."

"Mamm went over there? What did she say? Did it pass inspection?"

"Of course not." He grinned at her.

Which, unfortunately, made her smile, too.

Before she remembered that she wasn't going to smile at him so easily anymore. "Well, um, I was just going for a walk."

"So I see." Aden's expression hardened.

Christy raised his brows. "I don't think we've met before. Name's Christopher Fisher."

"Aden Reese."

"And you are one of Christina's friends?"

"I'm a little more than that."

Christina inwardly winced. How did one describe Aden? "Aden lives with us. With my family. He's almost like a brother."

Christy relaxed. "Oh. A brother. That's *gut.* For a minute there I thought you were a suitor."

"I do live with Christina and her family, but I am nothing like her *bruder.* At all."

Christy's eyes widened. "Ah. I think I'm beginning to understand now."

"I hope so," Aden said as he reached out and clasped her elbow.

"Aden!"

"I'm sorry, but your walk was over, right?"

"Well . . ."

"Because I told your *mamm* that I'd take you home." Before either she or Christy could reply to that, Aden continued.

"So, we should probably get going. We don't want anyone to worry."

Christina wasn't sure if she wanted to yell at Aden or laugh. "Christy, I'm sorry to cut our walk a little short."

"Are you sure you want to leave with him? I mean, I could take you home."

"I think not," Aden said before she could reply. "Taking Christina home should be a job for family."

"Or even almost family, it seems," Christy said, his voice dry.

"Thank you for taking me on the walk," she said softly before letting herself be dragged away by Aden.

The other man barely had time to raise a hand in farewell before Aden directed her down toward the livery.

When they'd walked half a block, she looked up at him. "Aden, you were mighty rude. What was that all about?"

"It was exactly as I said. I told Martha that I'd take you home."

"And?"

"And I thought someone in your family should meet a man called Christy."

"If you thought that way, you shouldn't have come to get me. As we've discussed, you are not family."

"I am definitely not your brother, but I know you well."

"And?"

"And I care about you, that's what."

"Do you? Or are you just biding time until you and your English nurse become serious?"

"Janice has nothing to do with this."

"Christy doesn't, either."

"Good."

Christina sighed. Part of her was more than ready to ask him a hundred questions. To ask him for some explanations. To ask him why he'd been so possessive and rude to Christy.

But instead she kept her silence. She was pretty sure that there was more to his story than he was prepared to tell her or she was prepared to hear.

Since Aden seemed just as content to keep his thoughts to himself, she imagined he was feeling the very same way.

chapter eighteen

For at least an hour, Judith had considered talking to her parents about everything that Bernie had told her. She'd actually thought about asking everyone in the family to come over and help her decide what to do. Though they might get excited and talk too much, they were also level-headed. Judith knew she would respect their opinions, especially Joshua's.

Most likely, they would offer good advice as well.

But in the end, she decided against getting everyone involved. Just like with their decision about adoption and agreeing to being foster parents, she knew the right answers could only come from Ben and herself.

What they were going through was so difficult, so personal, she didn't know if she had the strength to pretend she was braver and more hopeful than she was.

This was also a time to rely on the Lord's wisdom as well. He had led her and Ben to finally admit their love for each other. Actually, He'd led all of them through some very difficult times, holding them securely, letting them lean on Him when it felt as if they couldn't stand easily on their own two feet.

This felt like another time when the Lord was simply waiting for her to reach out to Him.

And so she prayed. She prayed and talked to God while holding a sleeping James.

Then, at last, she sat across from her husband and asked his advice with both an open mind and open heart.

"I was wondering when you were going to want to talk about things," Ben said when she'd finally broached the subject.

"I've been praying. Trying to find the right words. And praying for two open ears, too," she added with a wry smile.

Ben smiled gently. "Hearing that makes me feel better. I am mighty glad you have been praying so much."

"Because you knew I needed His help?"

"Because I knew we needed all the help we could get. So, what do you think, *mein lieb?*"

Feeling suddenly free, as if nothing she said would be judged or discounted, she began to talk. "I'm not sure. One minute I feel like we need to visit Kendra at the prison. The next minute I'm too afraid."

"What are you afraid of? Is it visiting a prison?"

"That's part of it. Going to a women's prison scares me. But that's not what I keep thinking about." Knowing she couldn't keep her worst fears a secret anymore, she said, "So far, I've been able to pretend that James's mom is just a stranger. A person who gave birth to him, but almost didn't matter." She winced. Even to her ears, her words sounded cruel.

"What I'm trying to say is that I'm afraid when we take James to see her, she's going to realize she made a mistake and won't want us. And I'll realize that I really am only a temporary person in his life."

"Actually, I've been thinking a lot of the same things. It was one thing when Bernie simply showed up with James. But now? Now we're going to be reaching out to Kendra—

and asking for her to trust us. I don't want to say or do the wrong thing."

"I have even wondered what's going to happen if James doesn't like us anymore. Even though I know it's silly, I'm afraid he'll remember her and we'll seem like strangers to him." She bit her lip. "I'm sorry. I know I sound selfish."

Ben shook his head. "*Nee*, Judith. You sound honest. And that, I think, is how we need to be. I'm glad we're talking about everything. Good or bad, it needs to be said."

They continued their conversation, weighing options and fears and hopes all afternoon and long into the evening. They discussed their concerns as they were feeding and later bathing James.

And continued to discuss Bernie's advice while cleaning the kitchen and cooking supper.

Finally, they pushed each other to make a decision when Judith was rocking James to sleep in her mother's rocking chair. "It's time," Ben finally said. "We need to make a decision."

"I know."

"What do you want to do? Meet with the aunts or visit Kendra?"

With a glance over her shoulder at the oak clock that her parents had given them on their first wedding anniversary, she said, "You tell me what you think first. "

Leaning forward, he braced his elbows on the table. "All right, here goes. Something tells me that we should pay a visit to Kendra first. Initially, I thought it would be easier to simply visit with Kendra's sisters, but I don't think that's the right thing to do.

She exhaled in relief. "I was thinking the same thing. After all, James is her baby. Even though she is in prison, she is still his mother. I don't think that bond can ever be broken."

"What Kendra wants should matter the most. And as much as it pains me to say it, Bernie did say the court would listen to Kendra's wishes first. I just hope we make a good impression with her."

"All we can be is ourselves, Judith," Ben reminded her.

"But if Kendra doesn't like us, she could ask her sisters to care for James."

"If that happens, we'll need to abide by that. We need to give all our doubts up to God, Judith." Ben walked to her side and placed a comforting hand on her shoulder. "Don't forget, He knows what is best for the baby."

"I know you are right." She sighed as she rested her head against her side.

The decision had been made. They would pay Kendra a visit, be themselves, and hope for the best.

And everything else? It was in the Lord's hands.

Aden wasn't sure why, but grilled ham and cheese sandwiches always tasted better at one in the morning.

For most of his life he'd been an erratic sleeper. He couldn't remember the last time he'd fallen asleep in the evening and didn't open his eyes until morning.

The only thing that really helped was a nighttime snack. When he was little, he'd become quite adept at sneaking out of his room, trundling down the hall, and snacking on an apple or a handful of cookies. If his parents ever suspected his nighttime wanderings, they never said.

Martha Kempf, on the other hand, had caught on right away. She'd followed him into the kitchen during his third foray into her pantry, practically scaring him out of his pants in the process.

But after learning that he was merely hungry and not upset, she'd taken to making sure he had all of his favorite midnight snacks on hand.

Sometime around his fourteenth year, he'd developed a passion for grilled ham and cheese sandwiches and the craving had stuck. Before long he'd become a master at creeping into the kitchen, lighting the small kerosene lamp that Martha always set out for him, and quickly and competently preparing his favorite treat.

There was a method to his madness. Both slices of bread had to be wheat. Brown mustard needed to coat one of them. Next he would put on two slices of white cheddar from Heini's cheese shop—sliced thin, thank you very much. Last he added two slices of smoked ham. When everything was just so, he would melt butter in Martha's favorite cast-iron pan, then cook his sandwich until it was crispy and perfectly toasted. Cutting the sandwich into fourths was his finishing touch.

Then he'd pour himself a tall glass of cold milk and dig in, enjoying the silence of the big house. Enjoying the opportunity to eat his treat completely by himself.

Joe had once tried to talk to him about his unusual habit. He'd even gone so far as to suggest that it wasn't natural.

Aden agreed.

But still, at least two or three times a week, he awoke hungry. When he got older, and was mature enough to analyze it, Aden figured that maybe these late-night sandwich sessions were his way of gaining control in his life. He'd lived most of his life dealing with the consequences of everyone else's actions. First, his parents had been too busy for him. Then they'd died, leaving him feeling completely lost and alone.

Then he'd gone from being an only child to the adopted one in a family with five children.

And then, of course, there was the vivid memory of Christina falling through the ice. He still dreamed about it, even after all these years. He doubted he'd ever completely forget the panic he'd felt when he'd gazed into the dark water and couldn't find her.

He thought about all of this as he walked down the hall just after one in the morning, his stomach and his head leading him to the kitchen. Just like always.

Until he realized the kerosene lantern was already lit.

Curious, Aden picked up his pace, only to come up short when he discovered who was already sitting at the kitchen table.

Christina looked up when he entered. "Ah. I was just sitting here, wondering if you were going to get up to cook tonight."

"I was planning on it," he murmured, surprised that she was acting as if her being up was a usual occurrence, which it definitely was not. "Why are you up? Are you sick?"

She shrugged. "I'm fine. Just couldn't sleep."

"So you decided to sit in here at the table?"

"Call me crazy, but I'd rather sit here in the light than next to Treva in the dark. There are only so many hours I can lay idly while listening to my sister snore."

He grinned. "I dare you to tell Treva she snores."

"I dare you!"

"No way. I value my life."

They shared a smile. His insides warmed as he realized how much he was going to miss living in the same house as Christina. They'd always been able to tease and joke with each other.

He was about to tease her some more when he noticed the shadows under her eyes. And realized what had actually woke her. A slow, sinking feeling settled in his gut and held on tight. "Did you have another nightmare tonight?"

After a moment's hesitation, she nodded.

"Want to talk about it?"

"There's no reason to. It was the same dream I always have."

"The one about us skating?"

"*Jah*. We skate, I trip. Then I fall through the ice."

"And what happened next?"

"You know what happens next." She grimaced. "Then I can't breathe."

There was such pain in her eyes, he yearned to take her in his arms and hold her tight. "But then I pull you out, right?"

She shook her head. "That's not what happens in my dreams. In my dreams I don't get free."

It made no sense but he was offended. "Why in the world don't I help you in your dreams? I did when it happened."

"I don't know. Maybe it's because I always panic in my dreams."

Quietly, he asked, "What happens next in your dream?"

She hung her head, her long hair sliding along her cheek and half covering her face. "Then, just as I'm about to die, I wake up."

"We need to do something about this, Christina. You shouldn't be dreaming such things. It's unhealthy."

"Hush. You and I both know that there's not much I can do. A person can't help one's dreams, right?"

Needing to touch her, he reached out and lifted her chin with his fingers. "You okay now?"

"I'm fine."

Moving to the refrigerator, he said, "Want a sandwich?"

"I do, if you're making grilled cheese."

"What else would I be making?" he joked. Pulling out his favorite jar of brown mustard, he said, "Do you want mustard and ham?"

"Of course. There's only one way to eat it, right?"

"Right." Happy to have something to do with his hands, he began pulling out everything he needed. "So what's going on with that farmer? With Christy?"

She wrinkled her nose. "Honestly, Aden. Couldn't you at least try to say his name in a nice way? You pronounce his name like it's a curse word."

"I don't believe you've ever heard me curse."

"Oh, stop. You know what I mean."

"Sorry. I can't help myself. I didn't like him."

"Of course you didn't like him. You don't even know him."

He stopped slathering butter on one of the slices of bread he'd just sliced long enough to point out the obvious. "You don't know him either, Christina."

She rolled her eyes. "That is exactly why I was walking with him. So I could get to know him. As I tried to tell you. Several times."

"Well, he seemed like a jerk."

"If he did, he was in good company."

"Ouch. That's a little harsh, don't you think?"

"Maybe. Or maybe not." She slumped. "Aden, I'll be surprised if he ever comes back to the Sugarcreek Inn. I think you put him off with your scowl."

He'd never admit it aloud, but he was pleased about that. Pulling out a fresh knife, he flipped over two of the slices of bread and began coating them with mustard. "I hope he was taken aback. He was being far too familiar with you, Christina. If he really liked you, he should have asked to call on you here. He should have wanted you to be safe and happy here. With your family looking over you."

"Oh, please."

Okay. He had to admit that he did sound a bit over-the top. But he was right. "Christy, there's nothing wrong with showing your parents respect."

"My parents were fine with his invitation. Or have you forgotten that you heard about my exciting, dangerous walk from my mother?"

"I haven't forgotten. But, still," he added, because he was trying to make a point. Even though he'd kind of forgotten what his point was.

Other than he didn't want Christina being courted by anyone.

"But still." She scoffed. "Like that means anything. But like I said, I probably won't see him again anyway."

"*Gut.*" He was glad he was facing the stove now so that she couldn't see his smile. Feeling mildly triumphant, he neatly placed the two sandwiches in the heated skillet.

With a grunt of impatience, Christina jumped to her feet and stomped to his side. Of course, her bare feet and fuzzy ivory-colored robe kind of ruined her obvious attempt to appear tough.

Actually, she looked a whole lot more like an angry angel than a fierce soul to be reckoned with. When she moved closer, smelling like she always did of vanilla and fresh rain, he ached to pull her into his arms and kiss her again.

Instead, he forced himself to continue to stare at the cooking sandwiches, as if the bread wouldn't toast if he wasn't there to watch it.

"Aden," she whispered. "For a couple of days now, I've been waiting for you to bring something up."

"And what is that?" he asked, kind of proud of the fact that he almost sounded unconcerned.

"You know what. Our kiss."

No, it wasn't "kiss," singular. It was *kisses*, plural. And with that small correction, the memory of how she'd felt in his arms, the way her lips had felt against his, returned in a flurry.

Not that the memory had ever been all that far from his thoughts. Swallowing hard, he felt his cheeks flush, whether from guilt or desire, he wasn't entirely sure.

He turned off the burner and pushed the pan toward the back of the range.

She stepped closer still. Now she was so close that her shoulder brushed against his arm. Close enough that if he wished, all he had to do was turn only the slightest bit in order to pull her to him.

"Aden, don't you think we should talk about what happened?"

His mouth went dry. And just like that, he realized he'd lost all control of the conversation. All he wanted to do was kiss her again. Right that minute. Right there in her parents' kitchen.

"Aden?"

"*Nee*," he blurted.

"*Nee*, what?"

Had her voice become softer or was it only his imagination? He cleared his throat. "There's no reason to talk about, um, what happened. Because you and I both know it shouldn't have happened."

"I think differently," she countered. And then, before he could attempt to come up with anything else to say, she continued. "Actually I'm glad we kissed."

"You are?"

"I am. Because, you see, that kiss . . . it wasn't brotherly, Aden. I was correct when I told Christy that I don't think of you as my brother. I never have. The way you kissed me proves that you don't think of me as a sister. Or even just as a friend."

No, he definitely did not. But this wasn't news to him. "We have already agreed that was a mistake."

"Do you really think it was?" Before he could answer, she continued, speaking a little faster, her words rolling one over the other off her tongue. Sliding into his consciousness. "Because you know what I think? I think it wasn't a mistake. I think you liked holding me in your arms, and I think I liked it, too."

He hadn't liked holding her. He'd *loved* it.

But of course he couldn't admit that.

As he fumbled for the correct words, realizing that there were none, she smiled at him softly.

"Aden, I think everything that's been happening is all connected. I think that's why you're seeing that English nurse now. I think that's why you decided to move away. I think that's why you are glaring at suitable suitors and pulling me away from them."

Feeling suddenly awkward and more than a little put on the spot, he grabbed a spatula and scooped up the two sandwiches from the skillet. "Grab me a plate, Christy."

She handed him the plate, then smiled softly. "That's why you didn't like Christopher, isn't it? Because his nickname is what you usually call me."

He was so flustered he feared that his hands were shaking as he arranged one of the sandwiches on the plate and then cut it into perfect squares. "Here is your sandwich."

"Aden, I deserve an answer."

So many words spun in his head. Excuses and lies. Secrets and valid reasons. He felt like he was living in the inside of a pinball machine he'd once seen in a train station, and petrified that he was going to blurt the wrong words and lose everything that was important to him.

"Yes," he finally admitted.

She leaned back. Stared at him. "Yes to what?"

"Yes to everything. Yes to being jealous. Yes to wanting to hold you in my arms again. Yes to you being the only person in the world I want to call Christy. Yes, to everything, Christina," he said, finally allowing himself to reveal every bit of frustration and pain.

"But the thing of it is, what I want doesn't matter, " he added.

"Of course it does."

"I don't think so. You and I can't have a future. I owe your parents everything. And they think of me as a son. I'm not going to repay their kindness by preying on their daughter," he said adamantly, taking his sandwich and sitting at the table.

"Is that what you would be doing? Preying on me?" she asked, joining him at the table.

No. He would be loving her. Cherishing her. Taking care of her. Kissing her—and more.

"*Jah*," he muttered, suddenly scraping back his chair and getting to his feet. And stomping off, leaving that grilled ham-and-cheese sandwich that always tasted so good on the plate. Untouched.

And he knew right then and right there that he would no longer be able to make another sandwich without thinking of her. Without thinking of her and remembering that he'd looked her in the eye and lied through his teeth.

chapter nineteen

The kitchen fell silent as the sounds of Aden stomping back to his room at the far end of the house faded into the distance. Sitting in front of the two plates loaded with perfectly cooked grilled ham-and-cheese sandwiches, Christina was tempted to chase after him.

She didn't understand why he'd run off from their conversation, but she had an idea that a strong sense of fear had a lot to do with it. Aden was afraid for things between them to change.

Stewing on that, she pulled one of the plates closer, picked up one of the squares, and took a bite. Immediately, the sharp tang of brown mustard, combined with ham, creamy cheddar cheese, and buttered toast filled her senses.

No one could make a sandwich like Aden. She closed her eyes and took another bite.

For the first time in her life, she felt as if she had the upper hand in their relationship. Aden was filled with fear and doubts. She, on the other hand, felt only hope for their future.

They had a long, abiding friendship and a history of being there for each other. They'd survived her awkward years and his *rumspringa*. Surely they could survive this moment, too?

Quietly, she closed her eyes, intending to belatedly give thanks for the sandwich. Then she felt a soft wave of happiness rush through her. And she realized that the Lord was with her.

Once again He was with her, helping her realize that He was in control of things and He was the one who had chosen this to be the right time for them. The right time, and that they were the right two people to be together.

A giggle erupted, just as she was chewing the last square of her sandwich. Everything was going to turn out all right.

"Christina?" her mother said as she stepped into the kitchen and stared at her through a pair of bleary eyes. "What in the world are you doing in here?"

"Eating a grilled ham-and-cheese."

Her mother turned to the stove and looked at the used—but unwashed—pan. Then at the sink, which contained the two knives.

And then at the untouched sandwich that Aden had left on the table.

"I should have guessed. I've certainly seen this evidence enough times." She sat down. "Where is Aden?"

"He decided he wasn't hungry after all."

Her mother's eyes brightened. "So no one is going to be having this one?"

"Only you, if you want it."

"I would never pass this up." After eating one of the squares in two bites, her mother said, "No one makes these like Aden. I'm going to miss him."

"Me, too, Mamm."

Holding a second square in her hand, her mother leaned her head back against the wooden rungs of the chair. "You know, I don't know how many times I've bought that boy ham, cheese, and that silly, fancy French mustard."

"At least hundreds of times."

"I know I've reminded him at least that many times to clean up his mess when he was done. He never learned."

"Aden's a mess. He always has been," Christina agreed.

"Sometimes, when I can't sleep, I'll listen for his steps in the middle of the night. My night is never complete unless I hear him opening up the refrigerator."

"The nights are sure going to become real quiet."

With a frown at the half of sandwich left on the plate, her mother stood. "You know what? I really shouldn't be eating so much in the middle of the night. I'm going to get indigestion or something."

Hiding a smile, Christina murmured, "I'll wash the dishes before I go to sleep."

With tears in her eyes, her mother shook her head. "Don't you dare. I've been washing up his mess for ten years. Tomorrow is going to be hard enough without not having that chore be the same."

As Christina watched her mother walk away, she knew it was time for some drastic measures. She wanted—no, needed—Aden to finally realize that they were meant to be together. And she needed to do it while he still lived with them. If she waited until he moved into his new apartment, she was certain he would avoid her as much as he could.

Racking her brain, she could only think of one thing that would change his mind about leaving the house, and about loving her.

She just hoped she would be strong enough to actually follow through and do what needed to be done.

"Got, You've gotten me this far," she whispered as she placed both plates on the counter by the sink. "I hope You know what You're doing, and that You're ready to watch over me real good. I need You now, because I know for sure and for certain that I can't handle what I'm about to do on my own."

And then, at long last, she turned off the lantern and padded back to her room.

There, she could slide into her rumpled bed, listen to Treva snore, begin to plan, and maybe even to dream.

But before she did any of that?

She was going to give thanks.

Jana had always thought she was far too practical a woman to care about red roses. They were expensive. Unnecessary. A bit clichéd. Maybe too grand a gesture.

But when Ross had shown up an hour ago with two dozen in his arms, she'd positively beamed.

Now, as they were sitting together in her sun room, she found herself gazing at those roses every couple of minutes. She'd put them in one of her favorite crystal vases. They looked beautiful and elegant. Special.

"I'm glad you like them, Jana," he said with a smile.

She felt her neck flush. "You caught me. I'm sorry, I can't help myself. They are so pretty. And such a surprise."

"If you want to know the truth, I kind of surprised myself. I was walking by Jones Florist and saw some in their refrigerator case and went on in. Bethany said you'd love them."

Jana privately thought Bethany Jones would say anything she could to sell two dozen roses, but she didn't blame her one bit. If their situations were reversed, she probably would have done the same thing. "I do love them. Have I thanked you?"

"Only about five times." He leaned forward, his elbows

on his knees. It was a familiar look now, one Jana privately called his "guy pose." "So, are you ready?"

"For the big event?" She shook her head. "Nope."

His tender look turned concerned. "You look worried. Are you?"

"A little."

"Jana, what do you think is going to happen?"

"Well," she said sweetly, enjoying their teasing conversation, "I think those four children of mine are going to descend on me like a quartet of locusts. And then they're going to turn on you. They're going to ask too many personal questions, watch you suspiciously, and then either ignore you or stay by your side.

"Come to think of it," she added with a frown, "I should probably go ahead and apologize right now for their rudeness."

He laughed. "I'll be able to take some difficult questioning. Even from kids. I am a cop, you know."

"But my kids— especially when they're all together—can be kind of a handful." Feeling mildly ashamed, she added, "I can't even believe I'm saying this. Aren't all mothers supposed to think their children are perfect? Or at least wonderful? Especially when they're grown and financially independent?"

He laughed again. "I'm sure they are wonderful. You're their mother, you know."

This time she was the one chuckling "That line is almost as great as my roses."

"It wasn't a line. You are a special lady, Jana. I mean that sincerely." Looking a bit more serious, he said, "I want to meet them. And I want to know them, and I want them to know me, Jana. If what we have continues, they're going to be seeing a whole lot more of me in the future."

She knew his words weren't easy to say. As romantic as he

was, he was also a bit skittish and reserved, especially when it came to relationships. He'd confided that he'd never imagined he would fall in love twice.

So she gathered her courage and said what was on her mind. "I want us to continue, Ross. I really do."

Reaching out, he linked his fingers through hers. "Then we're going to get through the big event without a problem."

"They're coming in two days." Jana groaned. "I'm so excited to see them, but still so anxious." She wanted the kids to like Ross and to support her new plans. She sincerely hoped nothing would happen to mess everything up.

"It's going to go okay, Jana. And even if it doesn't, we'll be okay."

That promise made a world of difference. He was so right: Even if all kinds of problems happened, the two of them would still be okay.

"Just let me know when you want me to join you, Jana, and I'll be there."

Looking at their linked fingers, she nodded, secretly wondering what he'd say if she admitted that part of her wanted him around the whole time.

chapter twenty

To Judith's surprise, it had been relatively easy to make an appointment to see Kendra at the Maryville Women's Correctional Facility. Bernie had helped her by talking to the warden and all sorts of other people who needed to be advised of their appointment. But in the end, all Ben had had to do was call and schedule their visit.

What wasn't so much of a surprise had been how her whole family had been eager to help them. Her parents had even offered to watch James for the day. Then, when they'd discovered that James was coming along, they offered to go on the journey, too, saying that they could help with the baby during the drive.

As much as Judith would have liked their support, she rejected the offer. More than ever, she knew that she and Ben were going to need to go see Kendra on their own. She and Ben wanted both Kendra and Bernie to view them as capable, mature adults.

But that hadn't stopped them from welcoming Caleb, Rebecca, Josh, and Gretta to their house the evening before.

To Judith's pleasure, she soon realized that they hadn't come to dispense advice but to instead offer support and comfort. The four of them had brought food, cooed over James, and simply listened. Not a one of them had been anything but encouraging and supportive.

A little while later, her parents had shown up to do the same thing.

She'd been humbled by their unselfishness and support. Awed by their love. And yet, when she'd told Caleb how grateful she was at the end of the night, he'd burst out laughing.

Which had come as the greatest surprise. "What's so funny?"

"You are, Judith. All my life, you've been the one who has been so unabashedly free with her advice and bright ideas. Not me."

"That's not true."

Caleb stared at her hard, with his arms folded over his chest. These days he now towered over her. "Of course it's true. You've never been shy about telling me what you thought. And you were always sure you were right."

She felt her cheeks heat. "I guess you're right. Was I insufferable?"

"Of course not. You were just being Judith."

"Great." It was pretty embarrassing to know that she'd spent most of her life acting like a bossy know-it-all.

"Believe me. Now I appreciate your looking out for me. Someone had to keep all of us in line. Seven *kinner* is too much for any mother. Even our *mamm*."

"Caleb, I handled everyone just fine," her mother said with a sniff.

"Sorry, Mamm."

Taking pity on her brother, Judith said brightly, "Mamm, after being alone with James for only a couple of hours, I realized that being a mother is a lot of work! I'm beginning to realize that I never was near as smart as I thought I was."

"Better late than never I suppose," her mother teased.

While everyone chuckled, Caleb gave her a hug good-bye. "I'll be thinking and praying for you tomorrow," he whispered. "Don't forget that we're all going to be praying for you."

"I won't. I need your prayers."

As they all filed out the door, it was Joshua who gave her the best surprise. "Lilly Miller is coming over in the morning with her *daed* to take you and Ben to the prison."

"But we were going to hire a driver," Ben said.

"I started thinking that maybe you didn't need a stranger knowing so much of your business. Plus, it's going to be a long day. Lilly will be here at ten."

Judith had been too grateful to protest her brother's arranging it all without her input.

They'd gone to bed, sure that it would be their most restless sleep ever. But to Judith's surprise, all of them slept a solid five hours before James made his first peep.

Now, as Lilly's father pulled up to the prison's main entrance, Judith felt a tremor race through her body. "I'm a little scared," she whispered to Ben.

"I am, too. Visiting a prison was never something I thought I'd be doing."

"Me, neither."

After Mr. Allen talked with the guard, he turned to them. "I'm afraid since Lilly and I aren't planning to visit anyone, we can't go any farther. The guard said a bus will be here in a few moments to pick you up."

"How will we get back in touch with ya?" Ben asked.

Mr. Allen pointed to a nearby parking lot. "We're going to wait over here. When a shuttle bus comes this way and drops people off, we'll be looking for you."

Knowing it was useless to do anything but offer their

thanks, Judith did just that, then with James safely in her arms, she followed her husband out of the car and to the small cement platform where they were told to wait.

Two minutes later, the bus arrived. Judith felt a shiver run down her spine before she pushed it away. Now wasn't the time to give in to fear. She had the support of her family, of Lilly and her family, of Bernie, and most important, of the Lord. With all of that, how could she be anything but thankful?

Feeling lighter than ever in spirit, she stepped into the shuttle, certain that everything was going to be fine.

"You're all right, aren't you?" Ben murmured as they sat down on a pair of benches.

"I am. I am just fine. And James will be, too. I'm sure of it." She kissed his brow and readjusted his blanket.

As the shuttle headed toward the large brick building with very few windows, Judith hoped she was right.

Though it was early, Christina knocked on Aden's door. "Aden?" she called out softly. "Aden, are you awake?"

She heard a couple of rustles, a muted exclamation, and then, at last, he replied, "Christina? Is that you?"

To her chagrin, she realized she was nodding on the other side of the door. Feeling foolish, she raised her voice a bit. "*Jah*, it is me. Can I come in?"

"*Nee!* I mean, hold on a sec," he said in a garbled way. After another few seconds, she heard a drawer slam and more rustling, and then his door flew open.

He wore faded pajama bottoms and his favorite old, worn T-shirt. But it was his eyes that caught her attention. They were filled with worry. "What's wrong?"

"Wrong? Oh, not a thing." When his panicked expression turned confused, then piercing, she took a step back.

Obviously striving for patience, he ran a hand over his jaw, a jaw that she now realized was covered with a fine covering of rough stubble. "So you decided to wake me up for no reason?"

"Oh, I had a reason."

"Which is?"

"It's snowing."

Folding his arms over his chest, he raised an eyebrow. "And your point is . . ."

"It means that the pond will be perfect to skate on this morning."

Slowly, his arms dropped to his sides. "And why does that matter to you?"

It was time. Gathering her courage, she said, "Because I have decided that it's time I went skating again. Aden, will you take me skating this morning? Please?"

He blinked and opened his mouth, then bit back whatever he was going to say, gazing at her intently. "I'm sorry, but Christy, you're going to have to back up a bit and let me catch up. Why do you want to go skating? Just a couple of days ago you were too scared to even stand next to the pond."

How could she even begin to try to explain everything that had been spinning in her head? Measuring her words carefully, she said, "I've been thinking a lot about you leaving. About our conversation about the seasons, and how everything moves forward . . . even when we're not quite ready. I don't want to fear change anymore, Aden."

He shook his head. "That conversation was about me being old enough to move out of your parents' house. Your fear about going ice-skating is completely different."

"Maybe not."

"Christina, I'm right about this. You can't compare the two. Me moving has nothing to do with you being afraid of something."

"I think it's all the same. Aden, if you can move on, I can, too."

"I know. But I think we should wait until the time is right."

"I think that time is now." Feeling stronger by the second, she smiled. "That pond is always going to be there. I'm tired of avoiding it. I think it's finally the right time to conquer my fear of ice-skating. But . . . but I need you with me. Will you come with me, Aden? Do you mind helping me?"

His expression instantly softened. "Of course I don't mind. But—"

She interrupted him, not wanting to hear any more of his excuses. "I know it's a bother. I know I've probably depended on you for too much for too long. . . ."

"You haven't."

"Maybe you're even tired of looking out for me," she said in a rush, willing to say anything to get her way. "Maybe you—"

"I'm not," he interrupted.

Feeling like she might just get her way, she said, "Aden, the truth is that I need you for one last thing. Will you come skating with me this morning? I know I can't face the ice by myself."

His cheeks flushed. "I'll help you with anything, always. But I'm not so certain that this is the right time." His voice gentled. "Maybe you're wanting this for the wrong reasons."

"I think I am ready." She swallowed hard. She wasn't sure if she was or not. She wasn't sure about anything anymore, truth be told. All she did know was that very soon everything between them was about to change. "I want to be, anyway."

"There's no hurry."

"No, there is. Aden, in just a couple of days, you're going to move away."

His eyes lit up with amusement. "Christina, I'm not heading off to the jungle. I'm moving into an apartment in town. I promise, we can do this another day. Another day when you're more ready." Reaching out, he clasped one of her hands in between both of his and gently squeezed.

His skin was warm and callused and so very familiar. A lump formed in her throat as she imagined a time when he wouldn't be in her life. When he would be clasping someone else's hand.

And so, although she knew her voice was sounding a little too desperate, she said, "Please, can't we just get it over with? I already checked, you don't have to work today. I don't, either."

He frowned a little mutinously and looked as if he was about to slam the door in her face, then at last sighed. "I can't believe I'm saying this. But . . . all right."

"Danke!"

He let go of her hand. "No, wait. Before we do this, you have to agree to something."

"Anything."

"I'm not going to let you put on skates and instantly jump on the ice. If we're going to actually give this a try, we're going to have to do it gradually."

"What do you mean by 'gradually'?"

"I mean that at first we're going to simply sit on the banks. Only then, if you're feeling ready, will we stand at the edge in our boots."

"That is not skating."

He ignored her comment. "Then, if you still feel like

you're ready for skates—and I think you're ready, too, we'll give it a try."

She raised a brow. "And if you don't think I'm ready?"

"Then we'll wait a week or two." Brightening, he said, "I know. We could try again on Sunday after church."

"By then you'll have moved."

"I'll wait."

"What?"

He looked at her hard. Then, looking above her head, he seemed to come to a decision and finally spoke. "If you're serious about this, I'll wait to move until you conquer your fear."

"You'll wait to move away until I can skate across the pond?"

He nodded. "But that doesn't mean I don't want to move. It's just that . . . if something happens . . . " His voice drifted off, letting her understand that this exercise wasn't going to be hard only for her, but for him, too. He was also battling his own demons and fears about her accident from ten years ago.

"If something happens, you'll be able to stay here, too," she added so he wouldn't have to.

"Jah." He exhaled. "Now, let me finish getting dressed. I'll meet you outside by the barn in ten minutes."

"I'll be ready."

"Me, too." He smiled weakly, then shut the door.

And then reality set in. She was going to have to face her fears before she could move forward.

It was frightening and exhilarating.

It was also going to be the hardest thing she'd ever done.

chapter twenty-one

Everything in the prison smelled like disinfectant, sweat, and something Judith couldn't quite put her finger on. Maybe it was regret?

In any case, she noticed the smell almost as much as the pale yellow walls, ugly beige linoleum flooring, and the many fierce-looking guards standing everywhere. She and Ben had had to walk through a metal detector and been searched, too. Then her purse had been placed in a locker before they'd been told to sit in some kind of awful waiting room filled with two rows of orange plastic chairs lining each wall, each one carefully nailed to the floor.

Luckily, she'd been able to keep a bottle, pacifier, and stuffed toy for James. Not that he seemed to be in need of anything, she realized with some relief. As usual, the baby seemed to be perfectly content to be held in her arms.

"Why do you think they nail the chairs to the floor?" she asked as they sat down. "It ain't like we could cart one off with all the guards here."

"It ain't like we'd want to," Ben said. Looking around them with a frown, he added, "I have no idea, but I think it would be best if we don't ask any questions."

"Oh, I won't. These chairs are the least of my worries. I hope James keeps being so good."

"If he cries, we'll cross that bridge when we come to it."

Looking down at the baby, Ben smiled. "Right now, it looks like he's handling this visit better than we are."

She chuckled. "I'm a nervous nelly."

"Yes, you are. But I'd be surprised if you weren't," he said in his gentle way. "This is hard."

Just as Judith nodded, the guard who she'd come to understand was the woman in charge, called their names and motioned for them to come forward. "This is it," she murmured, wishing she hadn't been so stubborn and let Bernie come with them.

"You will be sitting on one side of a plastic partition and the inmate will be sitting on the other side. You'll be using telephones to talk. Understand?"

"*Jah*," Ben replied.

"Then you all may walk to cubicle eight."

Judith looked around the room. There were ten cubicles taking up most of the room. In the center was a thick clear, plastic partition. Bold black numbers were pasted at the top of each, and old and dingy-looking black telephone receivers rested on either side on some kind of table that was attached to the partition's walls. There were also more orange chairs for people to sit in.

Currently, five of the cubicles were filled. Each person had a receiver held up to his or her ear and was talking eagerly to a woman in an orange uniform on the other side.

Judith had been afraid their appearance would cause a lot of commotion. Sometimes folks could be so rude and obtrusive around an Amish person, staring and asking nosy questions.

But here it was obvious that the only thing that interested anyone were the people they were talking to. They could have been invisible.

At last they got to cubicle eight, and Judith got her first look at Kendra, who was already sitting on the other side.

Kendra was solemn-looking and slim. Far slimmer than Judith had imagined. After all, she'd only given birth to James a few weeks earlier.

She also looked tired and wary, and was staring at Judith and Ben with a curious expression. Not because they were Amish, Judith realized. No, it was because they were taking care of James.

Judith knew the instant Kendra caught sight of James's face. Her whole demeanor transformed. A sweet smile played across her lips and her eyes lit up.

And even through the plastic barrier, Judith could feel Kendra's spirits lift.

Judith smiled politely as Ben helped her to her seat and then took his own beside her. They'd already agreed that she would be the one who talked on the phone. Bernie had suggested that Kendra might feel more comfortable talking with another woman instead of a strange man.

After sending out a silent prayer for guidance, Judith picked up the phone. "Hello, Kendra?" When the woman nodded, she continued. "Hi. My name is Judith. This here is my husband, Ben. We've brought James to see you for a visit."

"Hi." Her eyes darted to Ben and Judith before going right back to James. "How's he doing?"

Beside her, Ben rearranged the baby in his arms so Kendra could see him as well as possible. "He is doing real *gut*. He's a wonderful *boppli*, Kendra. A *wonderful-gut* little boy."

"He looks real good."

Kendra's voice was deep and scratchy. Judith thought she sounded a little wistful, too.

"I've really enjoyed getting to know him." Imagining that Kendra would probably like to hear as much about James as possible, Judith said, "He's a happy guy. Unless he needs his diaper changed! Then he fusses like nobody's business."

As Judith hoped, Kendra laughed. "But other than that, he's a joy. Always, he's been a joy for us to watch over."

Kendra's eyes lit up, making her appear younger. Softer. "Really?"

"Oh, *jah*. He's a real good eater, too. And he sleeps *wonderful-gut*, too."

Kendra smiled. "That's real good to hear. It's, ah, real nice of you to come up here to show him to me. And to tell me about him."

Judith smiled. After telling Kendra a few more stories, she knew it was time to get to the point of their visit. She knew she needed to tread carefully, however. She didn't want to cut Kendra's moment of happiness short. But when James fell sound asleep, and Kendra kept the phone to her ear and continued to stare at them in an expectant way, Judith knew that she couldn't put things off any longer. "Kendra, I am glad to know you. I'm glad for the chance to tell you about James, too. But there's another reason I . . . I mean, me and Ben wanted to see you. We need to talk to you about something."

She leaned forward. "What is it? Is something wrong with James?"

"Oh, *nee*. I mean, no. Nothing like that. It's rather about your sisters. Bernie—that's our social worker—I think you've met her?" After Kendra nodded slowly, Judith said, "It turns out that your sisters told Bernie that they're not real happy about us taking care of James."

"Why?"

Judith looked at her husband. When Ben shrugged, saying without words that she was doing fine, she continued. "It sounded like they wanted relatives to watch over him." When Kendra still looked a little muddled, she added, "Or maybe they'd rather have folks who, um, look more like James. What I mean to say is, um, we're Amish."

Through the Plexiglas window, Kendra stared at them, looking momentarily stunned. Then, to Judith's surprise, she started to chuckle. "I'm sorry," she said, waving a hand in the air, "but that struck me as funny. I promise, I knew exactly where James was going. When I was a little girl, my school took us on a field trip to an Amish farm." Her voice turned wistful. "It was so peaceful there. In the country. You could see for miles, and everything was so green. There was lots of room for a child to run and play. Is that what it's like where you live?"

"Yes." Judith had never thought about looking at her hometown through another person's eyes, but Kendra's description seemed fitting. Sugarcreek was a peaceful place. "It's a mighty nice place for *kinner*. To be sure."

"That's what I thought. I also remember the people we met. They were quiet and polite. Everything around them seemed so calm. Happy. But the most important thing I remembered was everyone's faith. One Amish lady said she lived by her faith every hour of every day. When I heard that, I knew I wanted to go back one day."

Excited that they had something in common, Judith leaned forward. "Did you go back again? What town was it? Was it Sugarcreek?"

Looking regretful, Kendra shook her head. "Nah. I grew up. And for a time, I forgot all about living peacefully. Actually, I started thinking that no one really lived like that. That

I must have made it up. Things happened. I hung out with the wrong crowd and then I really made a mistake with the wrong man." Her voice lowered. "One thing led to another." She rolled her eyes. "And then another. And now I'm here. I was sentenced to eight to ten years. There's a chance I might get out earlier, but even so, that won't even be a possibility for a couple of years."

"I'm sorry."

Kendra's brow rose. Then, miraculously, a small, sad smile lit her features as she stared at James. "Me, too. Seeing my baby so close. It's hard, you know?"

Feeling on the verge of tears, Judith nodded.

"What do you need me to do for you to keep my boy?"

"Bernie said you'll have to sign some more papers. These would state that you want James to stay where he is. Would you be willing to do that?"

Hardly taking her eyes off James, Kendra nodded slowly. "Yeah. I'll do that."

"Five minutes," the guard intoned.

It was time. Judith leaned forward, anxious to put as little space between herself and Kendra as possible.

She didn't care about why Kendra was in jail or that they were so different from each other. No, all she really cared about was comforting the woman who looked so sad and lost that Judith could almost feel her pain.

And right at that moment she finally understood what she was sure her family and Bernie and especially the Lord had been trying to tell her. That everything wasn't all about her. That it was time to cast aside her selfish wants and start concentrating on other people.

For months now she'd only been thinking about her pain, about how she couldn't have a baby of her own. She'd been so focused on herself she'd forgotten that she was only one of many people who carried burdens in their hearts.

It had taken a visit to a prison and a small, slight woman to remind her what it really meant to love unselfishly.

With that in mind, Judith looked James's mother in the eye and poured out her heart. "Kendra, we came here to tell you how much we already love James. I know I'm not his *mamm*, you are. But I am anxious to continue to keep him for you, if you'll allow it. I'm not perfect, but I promise you I'll do the best I can for your baby."

"I know you will," she whispered softly. Taking a breath, she darted a wary glance at the female guard looming over them. "Listen, we're running out of time. But I want to thank you for bringing him here. I've been worried sick about my baby. You've eased my mind."

"Bernie told us that we can come once a month. We'll come back in a month."

"And I'll be waiting."

Judith didn't want to push, but she was so desperate, she threw all caution to the wind. "So, Bernie can give you the paperwork?"

She nodded. "Tell her that I'll sign whatever she needs me to. James is in good hands."

"Time to go," the guard said.

Kendra stood up. "Thanks for this. You coming here helped a lot," she said simply before following the guard out of the room.

Her hand shaking, Judith set the receiver down. "This visit wasn't what I expected," she whispered as Ben helped her to her feet.

"For me, neither."

After passing through the same security stations that they

had when they entered the penitentiary, they walked outside into the cold air.

The change in temperature woke James up. His chocolate-brown eyes popped open and he squirmed in Ben's arms. After a moment, he let out a little cry.

"It looks like he's ready to go home." Ben laughed. "And I'm more than ready to pass him back to you."

Judith took James gratefully, not caring that he was fussing and obviously ready to have his diaper changed and to get out of the bright sun.

For her, the sunlight and cold breeze felt rejuvenating. Things were going to be okay. She and Ben were going to be able to continue to watch over James. And now that they'd visited Kendra once, Judith knew she'd be willing to return every month so that Kendra could get to see her baby.

Just as Ben had predicted, Got had taken care of everything. She breathed in deeply, giving thanks for the moment. For the day.

For everything.

It was amazing how much easier it was to go to work when she didn't feel the whole burden of responsibility weighing her down, Jana reflected as she opened another box of gift items.

Pippa now seemed to have everything under control in the dining room. So much so that Jana had cut back her hours sharply. Today she was only planning to stay at the restaurant long enough to restock and organize the gift area.

When she'd put it in, she'd hoped it would bring in a little extra income, but mainly that it would serve to occupy her customers while they waited for a table.

It had really taken off and had in fact become one of the reasons tourists ate at the restaurant. Before Pippa had come in, it had started to feel like a pain in her neck. It was a lot of work, constantly rearranging and straightening the shelves. Restocking and ordering merchandise.

But now she was thankful to have such a mindless task. Otherwise all she would be doing would be gazing out the window and pacing nervously as she waited for her kids to show up.

She still couldn't believe that they'd wanted to come to the restaurant first thing.

She'd wanted to fix a light luncheon at home to celebrate their arrival. But each had been fairly vague about when they would arrive. And wonder of wonders—now that they knew the restaurant wasn't going to be a big part of her life anymore?

They wanted to meet there.

So, she was making herself stay busy while she watched the door and tried to contain her excitement. And tried not to worry about how they were going to like Ross.

Or how Ross was going to like them.

Or how she was going to manage to seem calm, cool, and collected when everyone was in the same room together.

Leaning down, she got out a rag and carefully wiped down a shelf before replacing two boxes of candles on it.

Then she heard the door open.

With a start, she turned around and saw both her eldest and her youngest standing there together, looking wonderful and perfect. "Jay! Nick! You came!"

Their laughter rang as she scrambled to her feet and ran around the counter. One after the other, they launched themself into her arms. And although Nick was a good six inches taller and Jay at least two, she knew nothing had ever felt so wonderful or as familiar. "I'm so happy to see you both!"

Jay smiled. "Mom, look at you! You look great!"

She gave a little bow. "That's sweet of you to say."

"No, I mean it. Mom, you look . . . happy."

Nick hugged her again and kissed the top of her head. "You really do, Mom."

Not wanting to think about how she'd probably spent far too many years looking unhappy, Jana grinned. "I am happy. I can't help but notice that you both seem surprised, though."

Jay shot a telling look her brother's way. "Well, the way Nick was talking, I thought you might have dyed your hair pink and were running around in spandex."

"Oh?"

Nick rolled his eyes. "Obviously, Jay is exaggerating."

Brushing a hand down her brown corduroys and red sweater, Jana said, "As you can see, I'm still wearing my same old outfits. I haven't ventured into the spandex department yet. Now, come on in! Come meet Pippa! And see the girls in the back." She looked around, frowning when she didn't see any suitcases or backpacks. "Where are your things? And where are the others?"

"Melissa and Garrett are coming in together. Nick picked me up from the airport. So, is Ross here?"

"No. He's at work now. But he said he'd stop by when he got off of his shift."

Jay's smile got bigger. "I can't believe you're dating a policeman, Mom."

"Well, we're just seeing each other a bit. Taking things one day at a time. He's a nice man, though. I hope you all will like him. . . ."

Nick wrapped an arm around her shoulder. "If you like him, I have a feeling we might like him, too."

Realizing that Nick had decided to keep an open mind, Jana felt pure relief course through her. Maybe this visit with the kids was going to go all right after all.

For the next hour, she introduced Nick and Jay to Pippa and shared the news about their partnership. Marla and Kirsten waited on them, bringing out soup and rolls, and then slices of pie.

Just as they were finishing their pie, her two other kids entered. Followed by Ross.

After the round of hugs, she bit her lip and plunged in. "Nick, Melissa, Jay, and Garrett, please meet Ross."

Melissa looked him over and then smiled broadly. "Your boyfriend."

The kids started giggling, as if they were twelve instead of responsible adults. Shaking hands, they talked to Ross, who visited with each one with ease.

Soon, they'd pushed some more tables together, and Marla brought out more coffee cups and two full pies, one apple and one peanut butter cream.

Before Jana knew it, she was serving pie and carrying on two conversations at the same time. Somehow Ross took the chair beside her. Every so often, his gaze would meet hers and he'd gently smile.

Just as if he met the grown children of women he dated all the time. Except she knew he hadn't. She knew that he'd hardly dated at all since he'd gotten divorced.

After another hour went by, they all stood up and got ready to drive to her house, Ross promising to join them there for pizza later.

Right after they said good-bye to Pippa and the rest of the girls, Jay sidled up to her and linked her arm through Jana's elbow. "It's going to be okay, isn't it, Mom?"

Looking around at the Sugarcreek Inn, which was not quite "her" restaurant anymore . . . watching her other children standing out by their cars, talking a mile a minute. And seeing Melissa hug Ross good-bye before he joined them later, Jana nodded.

"It is," she said, with only a bit of wonder in her voice. "I think everything is going to be just fine, after all."

chapter twenty-two

There was fear, and then there was fear of ice.

Christina darted a hesitant glance at the snow-covered pond, now looming in front of them. The small pond suddenly looked as big as one of the Great Lakes and twice as dangerous.

With effort, she tamped down the fresh burst of apprehension that gripped her like a vise. The last thing she wanted was for Aden to guess just how petrified she actually was.

But he'd already noticed.

Concern clouded his eyes as he gazed at her so intently she feared he could read her mind. "We don't have to do this, you know," he murmured. "I won't think any less of you if we turn around."

"I know." And she did know it. But instead of easing her mind, it actually made her feel worse. If it had only been a matter of being been afraid to disappoint him—if that were her only fear—she would gladly use that as her excuse to turn around.

But she wasn't worried about Aden's opinion at the moment.

During their walk from the house to the pond she'd stopped thinking of ice-skating as a way to keep Aden by her side for a little longer. Instead, she'd started realizing that she needed to do this for herself.

For ten years, she'd suffered through nightmares and insomnia. She'd avoided water and dreaded the winter. Over time her accident had taken on gigantic proportions. She'd stopped seeing herself as a twelve-year-old who'd had an accident to someone who had made a series of bad choices and almost killed herself and Aden with her foolishness.

Worse, instead of admitting that her problems were more than she could handle on her own, she'd kept everything inside and not sought help from her parents or Aden. She'd even been so foolish that she hadn't even asked the Lord for help.

But all that had done was make things worse.

Now, at long last, she was determined to face her fears. She was never going to be able to move forward in her life if she constantly blocked out the past.

She took a moment to attempt to put her jumbled thoughts in order, wanting to try to get him to understand what she was thinking—even if she didn't completely understand it all herself. "Aden, I think I do need to do this. Ten years is more than enough time to hold on to an unreasonable fear. Ain't so?" She'd added the last as a timid attempt to make him smile.

But instead of grinning, Aden remained stoic, staring at her intently. "We all have hang-ups, Christina. We all have fears that don't always make sense. It's nothing to be ashamed of."

"I'm not ashamed," she lied.

He winced. "Perhaps that was the wrong thing to say. What I meant was that we all have foibles and fears."

"Even you?"

"Especially me."

She yearned to ask him what his fears were, but she couldn't seem to concentrate on anything but the sight of the pond in front of them.

It loomed in front of her, looking, she supposed, like a beautiful centerpiece in a winter scene. It was still snowing, and the gently falling flakes swirled and danced in the air, finally coming to rest on the pond's surface.

She knew that later that day children from all around would venture to the pond. Soon the area would be scattered with boots and skates, abandoned coats and mittens. Laughter would ring out, flowing down the valley. Loud enough that she'd be able to hear it from her bedroom.

But now it was just the two of them.

As yet another shudder ran through her, Christina pushed it away. "Let's go. If we wait any longer, I'm going to chicken out."

"Christina, I told you, you won't be chickening out." Obviously trying to rein in his frustration, he tossed his skates on the ground. "Look. I know you wanting to get on the ice is all my fault. I'm so sorry I ever made you feel like there was something wrong with you."

"You didn't."

"We both know I did. The other day when we were walking home, I should have steered you clear of this place instead of forcing you to stand so close to the ice. I pushed you too hard and didn't listen to you like I should have. It was wrong of me. And callous."

"Aden, you were right."

Giving no indication that he'd heard her, he continued. "The fact is, I should never have made you do anything you were uncomfortable with. I'm no doctor or preacher or expert on fighting fears. I don't know what I was thinking. . . ."

"I do. You wanted to help me." She started walking, ignoring his sound of frustration. "Come on, Aden," she called out over her shoulder. "As of this morning, I'm done standing still. I'm moving forward."

Behind her, he sighed. "Lord help us all," he muttered as he bent down and retrieved his skates. Then, after a brief pause, he started following.

His final acquiescence should have given her a feeling of pleasure. Instead, now that she realized nothing else was holding her back, she felt as if she were free-falling. Rushing toward her fears with the speed of a freight train.

Finally moving forward.

She clung to the phrase with everything she had, repeating it silently in her head, over and over until it became the only thing she could concentrate on. She ignored the snow swirling around them, ignored the cold wind tickling her cheeks. Even ignored Aden's presence next to her.

All that mattered was that she wasn't letting her fear control her any longer.

Carefully she rearranged the skates on her shoulder. The white leather skates were Treva's favorites. She'd saved all winter for them. And to Christina's embarrassment, she hadn't even told Treva she was borrowing them.

Continuing, Christina strode across the frozen meadow and ventured up the slight hill that surrounded the frozen pond. She heard Aden's boots crunch on the snow behind her, his pace measured and steady. She cocked her head, ready to hear him offer advice or even another warning. But he didn't say a word.

He didn't even increase his pace so that he could walk by her side again. Obviously, he was letting her lead. Letting her make the next steps on her own. It was exhilarating, the idea that he trusted her enough to keep his silence. But it was scary, too. For the first time in their relationship she was with him, but not leaning on him.

Not until they got to the onset of the pond's banks did she stop.

She hadn't done it intentionally. Instead, it was as if her feet had elected to take control and froze.

Looming barely three feet in front of her, almost close enough to touch, the ice taunted her. And as every fear she'd cradled close to her heart gained strength, her body began to shake again.

Tears formed in her eyes. With a cry of dismay, Christina realized that there wasn't a thing she could do about it, either.

Suddenly, she was helpless all over again, as weak and terrified as she'd been all those years ago when she'd fallen through the ice and felt the bone-crushing cold, covered only by the panic of her terror.

Teeth chattering, she wrapped her arms around her waist and held on tight. "I've been such a fool, Aden," she whispered. "And I have a confession."

"What is it?"

"I . . . I did want to skate again for me. But this morning, I wanted to do it for you, too."

"Me? Why?"

"Because I . . . I wanted you to love me." She hung her head, too embarrassed to look at him. "I wanted you to think of me as someone who was mature. Strong. A woman you could be proud of."

"Christina, I am proud of you."

She shook off his words. "Now here I am, too scared to do anything but stand here and shake. Obviously, I'm not going to get any better, am I? This . . . this fear is as much a part of me as my dumb scar."

Just as she braced herself for his rejection, a warm, solid arm curved around her waist. "You don't ever need to do a thing to prove yourself to me. You never have." Cuddling her closer, he blew out a ragged sigh. "The thing is, I've loved you, too. I've loved you for most of my life. For as long as I can remember."

She squeezed her eyes tight. Trying to drink in his words and figure out what they meant, all at the same time.

Then she felt his lips brush the nape of her neck. And felt his strength flow into her. "I've got you, Christina," he whispered again and again. "I promise. I've got you. I've got you and I'm not going to let you go. Not now, not ever."

After the slightest of hesitations, she leaned back against his body. Felt how solid and strong he was. Felt his warm breath as it brushed her cheek.

"I've got you, Christina," he whispered again. "I've got you."

And in that moment, she knew it was true. Aden was going to help her, no matter what. If she decided to leave, he would be by her side.

If she dared to step on the ice, he was going to keep her safe. No matter what, he wasn't going to let her go through any of it on her own. And because of that, she knew she no longer had to be afraid.

And right then and there she knew that she was finally going to be able to do anything she wanted—because he already held the most important thing: her heart.

Aden's heart was pounding as he wrapped his arms more securely around Christina. He'd just given her everything he had. His heart, his secret, and the promise that he'd kept so carefully guarded for most of his life.

Little by little, he felt her body relax. He gave her a little squeeze, then released her with reluctance when he realized his hands were now what was trembling.

She noticed. Looking over her shoulder, she met his gaze. "Aden?"

"Sorry. I, ah, though I might have been holding you too tightly."

The emotion shining in her eyes went a little flat. When she took a step away, a dozen emotions fluttered through Aden's insides, desire warring with an overwhelming feeling of protection while worry and pride kept company in his heart

Never had he been so afraid. His mouth had surely gotten them to this place. Once again, he'd been thinking he knew everything when it was becoming more apparent by the second that he knew nothing. What was he going to do if she fell and got hurt, or if this experience only heightened her fears instead of easing them? The last thing he'd wanted to do was make her even more afraid of being on the ice.

But then he remembered hearing Treva say she'd gone skating yesterday after work. If she had skated on the pond just a few hours earlier, he knew it was safe.

Plus, as he stared at the ice, it looked as firm and solid as he'd ever seen it to be. It was as safe as it had ever been.

That bit of assurance eased his conscience and helped him regain his usual confidence. "What do you want to do?"

"I want to skate one time around the pond. Even if I never do it again, I want to know that at least one time I was brave enough to get back on the ice."

"Then that is what we'll do." He slid his skates off his shoulder and took the last two steps toward the snow-covered ridge. "Let's do this, Christina."

She nodded, then sat down on one of the rocks and methodically began switching out her heavy black winter boots for her sister's white leather skates.

As Aden laced up his own black skates, he was relieved to notice that her hands weren't shaking as she tied the white laces, taking care to double-tie the neat bow on each skate. "I'm ready," she said at last.

"All right, then," he said, inserting a bit of enthusiasm into his tone that he didn't feel. "Let me have your hand."

She slipped her palm right next to his. "Aden—"

"*Jah?*" he said as he planted one foot in the snow and pulled himself up.

"If I fall . . ." She bit her bottom lip, obviously too unsure how to verbalize what she needed to say.

And because he knew he loved her, he made a promise he could only hope the Lord would help him keep. "I won't let you fall."

"But if I do—"

"I won't," he interrupted as he pulled her up beside him. Summoning a smile, he met her eyes. "Remember? I've got you. Now, stop worrying and follow my lead."

Her steps were as wobbly as her smile as she got to her feet. Her grip, however, felt as strong as his own.

He'd never been so proud of her.

And as they stepped onto the ice, Aden realized two things. One, he was going to skate as if his life depended on it. And two? He now knew without a doubt why his life depended on it. Christina Kempf was his life. She always had been, from the first time he'd spied her. She always would be his life, too. And now that they loved each other, he knew she was his forever.

He didn't even care any longer if her family hated him

for falling in love with her. He'd waited too long for this moment. And just as he held her hand, she held his heart forever.

With a deep breath, he positioned one arm around her waist, his other holding her left hand securely. Then, at last, he said a silent prayer and pushed off with his right toe.

And like it had always been meant to be, they glided across the ice as one.

chapter twenty-three

Christina was learning that it was possible to see absolutely nothing with her eyes wide open. Her world felt like a black void, illuminated only by the wind blowing across her face and the mind-numbing realization that she was facing her greatest fear.

"You're doing it, Christy!" Aden called out. "*Gut* for you!"

His voice sounded like it came from the back of a long, windy tunnel. It registered in her brain but she still remained confused. It was truly as if her brain and her body were two separate beings. Little that she saw and felt made any sense.

All she was aware of as Aden led her across the ice was that she was surviving. She wasn't falling through the ice. She wasn't gasping for air as frigid water tried to choke her.

Then Aden laughed. The sound was filled with such joy that it jarred her from her stupor. She blinked once. Twice. And then finally allowed her eyes to focus.

What a sight was before her, too! The tree branches that surrounded them were covered with bright, sparkling snow. The air was crisp and smelled fresh and heavenly. Delicate snowflakes painted their coats and cheeks. And Aden was gazing at her with so much love in his eyes that it nearly took her breath away.

"There you are," he murmured. "For a moment there, I was afraid I'd lost you." His lips curved upward as he pulled her a little closer, easing her around the pond in a wide circle. The pace was just fast enough to keep them easily upright. Just slow enough to let her feel like she was in control.

"For a moment, I thought I had gotten lost. That I'd slipped into another dream," she admitted. "But now here I am, skating by your side. I can hardly believe it."

"I'm so proud of you, Christina."

"And I'm so thankful for you, Aden. You've given me a gift today. A wondrous gift. I don't know how I'll ever be able to thank you."

"I didn't do anything. It was your courage that got you here."

Not wanting to argue the point, she merely smiled. As they made another pass, she slowly let herself relax enough to allow her body to settle into an easy stride. But still she clung to his hand.

"Good girl. You look like a champion again," he teased.

"Hardly that. But don't let me go."

"Never."

His voice was so solemn, she tilted her chin up, met his gaze. And read the promise in his eyes. "You're talking about more than skating, aren't you?"

He nodded. "When I said I loved you, I meant every word. Did you?"

There was only one answer. "I love you, too, Aden. I've loved you for years. I've simply been waiting for you to feel the same way."

He chuckled. "It sounds as if we'd been a little bit braver we could have saved ourselves a lot of pain."

"Maybe so. Or maybe the Lord had always intended for this to be the right time."

"I think that's it. At last, this is our time, Christina. And though I may be rushing things too fast, I have to warn you that I want it all. I want you to be mine forever. I want to marry you."

"You want to marry me?"

"Uh-huh. And as soon as possible." He winced. "Did I speak too soon?" He stopped abruptly, obviously trying to gauge her reaction.

Taken off guard, she teetered on the blades of her skates, let go of his hand in order to regain her balance, and then promptly fell.

"Oh!" she cried, closing her eyes tightly and preparing herself to face her worst nightmares. But all that happened was that she landed with a *thud* on her backside. "Umph!"

In an instant, Aden was kneeling next to her. He reached for her and held her close. "Christina, are you all right?"

As she looked into his eyes, all the fears and doubts and pain drifted away in a bubble of laughter. She'd done it. She'd conquered her fears and had skated a full circle around the pond. Her worst fear had not come true. She'd fallen, but instead of crashing through the ice, she'd merely gotten a little jarred.

Aden loved her and he'd asked her to marry him.

"I don't know if I've ever been better!" she exclaimed, wanting to shout her happiness to the heavens. "Oh, Aden, look at us!"

Little by little, his tentative smile eased into a genuine one, and then was replaced by a low chuckle. Within seconds, he pulled her to him and kissed her.

And kissed her again.

It was miraculous. And magical. And life affirming. Making Christina realize that the Lord had been exactly right. For everything there really was a season.

Everything was going to be just fine. Aden and she were going to finally stop playing games and circling each other. Instead they were going to declare their love and begin to make plans to be together.

Already she could imagine how excited everyone was going to be about their news!

"Christina?" her father's voice reached them like the deep clang of a brass bell.

Startled, Aden broke apart from her and clambered to his feet. "Joe. And Martha. What a surprise."

"If you're surprised, I am shocked, Aden," her mother said. "And you, Christina? Why, I don't know what to say to you."

"Obviously you do," she muttered under her breath. Christina didn't trust herself to stand up quite yet. Instead, she braced herself on her hands as her parents strode forward.

As they marched closer, Aden reached down for Christina's hands. "Let me help you to your feet."

His voice was as gentle and silky as she'd ever hoped. And it gave her courage to clasp his hands and get back on the blades of her skates.

And as he helped her, she realized that she only had eyes for him.

Nothing else mattered.

chapter twenty-four

This was certainly a situation she'd never expected to be in. Her parents were standing on the edge of the pond, both looking angry enough to spit nails.

And here she was standing next to Aden in the middle of a frozen pond. Which, of course, was the absolute last place she'd ever dreamed she'd be.

The situation was so fanciful, Christina didn't know whether to laugh or cry.

She decided to keep silent and hope that Aden would know how to best handle the situation.

"What is going on, Aden?" her father asked. "When Treva told us her skates were missing and that she feared you took Christina skating, we could scarcely believe our ears. But this sight you treated us to . . . both of you lying on the ice, kissing?" His expression darkened. "I hardly know what to say."

Christina opened her mouth, more than ready to explain things. But before she had a chance to utter a word, Aden replied.

"What just happened is all my fault," he answered. "Christina asked me to help her conquer her fear of the ice and I agreed. But I should have asked you first."

Martha folded her arms over her chest. "Yes, you should have. Anything could have happened! Christina could have fallen again!" she exclaimed, each word practically shaking with emotion. "Or she could have gotten hurt. All sorts of things could have happened and we wouldn't have known. You shouldn't have kept this a secret, Aden. After everything we've given you, you've repaid us by betraying our trust."

"I realize that." Not meeting Christina's eyes, he stepped off the ice. "I am sorry," he told her parents. "It is obvious you are angry, and you have every right to be."

Still wearing a thunderous expression, her father glared at her. "Christina, do not think that you have gotten out of this discussion. We have not even started."

"*Jah*, Daed."

"Now, get off the ice, change out of those skates, and then come along. We will discuss your behavior at home."

A couple of things were preventing her from doing that. She didn't want to be dragged home like a wayward child. She certainly didn't want to follow her parents down the path toward the house, wondering all the while what was going to happen.

But more than anything, she realized that she wasn't in any hurry to leave Aden's side. She also had a bit of a problem. Without Aden by her side, she was a little afraid to skate off the ice. "I canna do that," she blurted.

Before her parents could comment on that, Aden turned around and skated back to her side. "What's wrong? Did you get hurt when you fell?"

"My body is okay, but everything else? It's not," she whispered. "This is ridiculous. We've come too far to be ordered to take off our skates and go back home. My parents are acting like I'm too young to know my mind."

"So you have no regrets?"

"Not a single one," she said with a smile.

Her father groaned. "Christina, if you're going to get all

upset and in a mood, I'd rather you did it in the kitchen. There at least we'll all be warm."

"Daed, Aden and I are fine. He and I will be inside in a moment. But I need you to leave us alone."

"Christina, are you sure about this?" Aden asked.

She looked into his eyes, and for the first time she saw an honesty there that gave her hope. "I'm certain. I'm more than sure."

After giving her a brief nod, he turned to her parents. "I'll bring Christina home in a little while."

Her father looked flummoxed. Martha looked stunned. "Are you ignoring our wishes, Aden?" she said.

"Not at all. I'm simply choosing to follow Christina's wants." He turned back to her. "Listen, I want to talk with you for as long as you want, about whatever you want. But not while standing out here on the ice. May I help you skate to the edge?"

Christina was afraid her legs were shaking too much to support herself. "*Jah.* As soon as we're alone."

Thankfully, they didn't have to wait too long. After few more grumbles, her parents walked away, their steps measured and slow.

When she was sure they were out of sight, Christina held out her hand with a laugh. "Now you can help me. But I have to warn ya, I think my legs are frozen stiff."

"I hope not. Your parents are mad enough at me. I can't let you get sick, too."

"I'll worry about them." She chuckled. "You worry about getting me off the ice."

Something new lit his eyes. "Hold on to me and hand me your foot."

Mesmerized, she did as he asked, then gasped as he started unlacing one boot. "Aden, what in the world?"

"Shh. Don't argue. Give me your other foot now."

Now feeling like she couldn't have ignored his wishes even if she'd wanted to, Christina straightened her other leg and let him unlace her boot.

Then she stood motionless as he carefully tied the laces together in a neat bow and walked them to the bank. When he returned, he murmured, "Lift your arms, Christina."

She lifted her arms. And then gave a little shriek as he swung her into his arms, cradling her close to his chest. Giggling, she wrapped her arms around his neck and held on tight. "Aden, be careful. I fear I'm too heavy for you to carry around."

"Never," he said as he easily glided to the side of the frozen pond with her in his arms. When he stopped, he looked down at her. "Do you feel better now?"

"*Jah.*" To be truthful, she wasn't sure how she felt at the moment. She was relieved and stunned. Astonished and happy. "You can put me down now."

Carefully, he repositioned his arms, then let her slide to the ground. "You'd best put your boots on, Christy."

She nodded, then did as he suggested as he switched out his own boots.

At last there was nothing else to do but talk. "What did you want to say?" he whispered.

"That I meant it when I said I loved you."

"I meant it, too. You're my girl now, Christina. You know that, right?"

"I know," she whispered. Because she'd always known it from the start. From the moment they'd met, he'd always had her heart.

She was just thankful that at long last their love was out in the open.

So very thankful.

Hand in hand they walked back to the house. Christina couldn't help noticing that the snowflakes no longer seemed ominous. Instead they were simply pretty reminders of the miraculous changes that had taken place between them.

Aden kept her hand nestled in his when they stepped inside. When they walked into the kitchen everyone was there waiting for them.

Her brothers looked at her and Aden curiously, as if they couldn't understand what the fuss was about. Leanna, being thirteen, had stars in her eyes. Christina could practically read her mind—Leanna was eagerly planning their wedding already.

Even Treva looked bemused. Christina knew her sister was going to be genuinely happy for her and Aden. Well, she would be, as soon as she got over the fact that Christina had kept her in the dark.

Her parents, on the other hand, were a different story. Her father seemed unable to look away from their linked fingers. And her mother was practically biting her tongue. It was obvious she had much to say.

She barely waited a full minute. "Do either of you feel compelled to tell us what's going on yet?"

Aden smiled. "Today is the very best day of my life. Christina here has just agreed to be my wife."

"I knew it!" Leanna announced. "Can I help you plan it, Christy?"

"Of course you can," she said softly. "Mamm, Daed, I am mighty happy. Will you join me in my happiness?"

Her mother crossed her arms over her chest. "And all this just happened? Just like that?"

"Hardly," Aden said.

"Your eyes might be full of stars, but we need more of an explanation, daughter," her father said. "We raised you practically as siblings."

"But I never thought of Aden that way," Christina said. "I've loved him forever. The truth is that this day has been years in the making."

Her mother raised her eyebrows. "That long?"

Carefully, Aden wrapped an arm around Christina, showing them that he felt exactly the same way she did. That they'd waited long enough. And that they were old enough to make up their own minds. "It's the happiest day of my life," he said, taking time to look each person in the eye. "I'd love it if you would be happy, too. Because, at long last, I would have it no other way."

"And you, daughter?" her mother asked. "What do you have to say about all of this?"

Christina took a breath, considering all the things she could say, then finally decided to speak from the heart.

"Only that I am thankful," she said at last. "I am so very, very thankful."

Turning away from her family, she looked into Aden's eyes. She saw love there, and the promise of a beautiful future together.

And that was when she realized that being thankful summed up her feelings.

In fact, it was almost more than enough.

epilogue

With a gasp and a cry, she opened her eyes, breathing deeply, taking in fresh, fortifying breaths like the counselor had taught her.

Bit by bit, the last remnants of her dream slid away, letting Christina Reese blink and focus on the present. As she became more aware of the soft flannel sheets that surrounded her, the faint scent of roses from the bouquet on her chest of drawers, and the warm sense of security that now glowed inside her, she knew she was at home, not in dark, brackish water.

She was sitting in her bed, warm and cozy in her favorite nightgown, the one that Treva had embroidered tiny pink flowers on.

She stretched her legs, happy that her breathing had already almost returned to normal. Her episodes were getting better and better.

Now, if she could only convince her husband to stay by her side through the night.

She knew where he was, of course. After slipping on her robe and slippers, she walked to the kitchen—and found Aden almost exactly where she'd imagined him to be. He was standing at the kitchen counter, contentedly buttering two slices of bread.

"Aden, I thought you were going to try to stop your middle-of-the-night wanderings."

"I would, if I didn't get so hungry." Setting his knife down, he examined her face more closely. "Another dream tonight?"

"Yep."

"I'm sorry I wasn't next to you."

The last time she'd had her nightmare he'd held her for hours afterward, whispering over and over that she was all right. "It's okay, it wasn't too bad this time."

"Really?"

"I woke up before things got too bad. And," she added proudly, "I didn't even start hyperventilating. I'm making big strides."

"That is good news." Walking over, he kissed her brow. "Congratulations. You're right, love. That is *wonderful-gut* progress."

"Now all we have to do is cure you of your need for grilled ham-and-cheese sandwiches," she joked.

He raised his brows. "So, wife, would you care for one?"

By now they almost had their own script. "Do you have mustard?"

Eyes sparkling, he picked up the jar of Grey Poupon. "Got it right here."

"Then my answer is yes, of course."

He grinned as he pulled out more bread and began making two sandwiches. She sat at their small kitchen table and contentedly watched Aden make yet another sandwich.

It had been a busy month. After finally admitting their love to each other—and to her family—things had moved forward like a roller coaster. Wedding plans began in earnest, with Leanna spearheading the arrangements.

They'd decided to move into his little apartment instead of building onto the main house, wanting to spend their first year of marriage in relative privacy.

In the middle of everything Aden and she talked more and more about that skating accident all those years ago. He forced her to tell her parents about her nightmares. And then, much to her dismay, all of them encouraged her to talk with one of the counselors at Aden's hospital.

Talking about things helped. All it took was a couple of sessions with the counselor to learn some ways to help her cope with her darkest fears.

And now, here they were, newlyweds, living on their own and enjoying the novelty of setting up their own home. And realizing that while so many things were different between them, much was basically the same.

"Here you go, Christy," Aden said as he slid a plate in front of her before sitting down with his own.

Just as it had always been, the first bite was the very best. "It's a good one tonight."

"Danke."

They chewed in silence for a few minutes, then Christy pushed her plate to one side. "So, why were you up tonight? You didn't have a bad dream, too, did you?"

"I just couldn't sleep."

"Oh? Were you worried about something?"

"Not at all." Standing up, he took her hand and pulled her up against him. "I woke up wide awake, and then made the mistake of counting my blessings as a way to get back to sleep."

"What was wrong with that?"

His expression turned bemused. "It just happens, I have a lot to thank the good Lord for. It takes a while. By the time I was done I got hungry."

Christina chuckled as she turned off the kerosene lamp. "I've never heard of someone having trouble sleeping because they were too happy."

"What can I say?" he quipped. "I'm a man in a million, Christina."

"That is true," she murmured as she led her husband out of the kitchen. He *was* a man in a million. The only man she'd ever wanted. "It's time we went to bed, Aden."

Smiling slowly, he nodded. "Christina dear, you read my mind. I just happened to be thinking the very same thing." She giggled as she led the way in the dark, knowing that even if he couldn't see her, he would follow.

Knowing she would never want it to be any other way.

About the author

2 Meet Shelley Shepard Gray

About the book

4 Letter from the Author

6 Questions for Discussion

8 Peanut Butter Pie

Read on

9 A Sneak Peek of Shelley Shepard Gray's Next Book, *Joyful*

Insights,
Interviews
& More . . .

Meet
Shelley Shepard Gray

PEOPLE OFTEN ASK how I started writing. Some believe I've been a writer all my life, others ask if I've always felt I had a story I needed to tell. I'm afraid my reasons couldn't be more different. See, I started writing one day because I didn't have anything to read.

I've always loved to read. I was the girl in the back of the classroom with her nose in a book, the mom who kept a couple of novels in her car to read during soccer practice, the person who made weekly visits to the bookstore and the library.

Back when I taught elementary school, I used to read during my lunch breaks.

One day, when I realized I'd forgotten to bring something to read, I turned on my computer and took a leap of faith. Feeling a little like I was doing something wrong, I typed those first words: *Chapter One*.

I didn't start writing with the intent of publishing a book. Actually, I just wrote for myself.

For the most part, I still write for myself, which is why, I think, I'm able to write so much. I write books that I'd like to read. Books that I would have liked to have in my old teacher tote bag. I'm always relieved and surprised and so happy when other people want to read my books, too!

Another question I'm often asked is why I choose to write inspirational fiction. Maybe at first glance, it does seem surprising. I'm not the type of person who usually talks about my faith in the line at the grocery store or when I'm out to lunch with friends. For me, my faith has always felt like more of a private thing. I feel that I'm still on my faith journey—still learning and studying God's word.

And that, I think, is why writing inspirational fiction is such a good fit for me. I enjoy writing about characters who happen to be in the middle of their faith journeys, too. They're not perfect, and they don't always make the right decisions. Sometimes they make mistakes, and sometimes they do something they're proud of. They're characters who are a lot like me.

Only God knows what else He has in store for me. He's given me the will and the ability to write stories to glorify Him. He's put many people in my life who are supportive and caring. I feel blessed and thankful . . . and excited to see what will happen next! ◠

Letter from the Author

Dear Reader,

It wasn't my finest moment. One afternoon, just a few days before Easter, my husband and I took our two children to one of the nicest malls in Dallas. The whole purpose? To have lunch at Neiman Marcus.

It sounds silly now, but back then, well, I needed a fancy lunch out. We had two kids under two, and I spent my days carting kids to day care, teaching school all day, and then doing laundry way too late at night. We didn't have a lot of extra money, and it seemed that every bit we did have went toward diapers and the hundred things two tiny children need. I was tired and stressed and pretty sick of wearing clothes with stains on them.

And so, one Saturday, my husband suggested we get dressed up and go out to a fancy lunch. We walked around the mall and window-shopped and daydreamed about actually getting a full night's sleep. All the while people looked into our double stroller at our cute kids. And then they did a double take.

Every time I saw someone look at our children just a little longer than normal, I lifted my chin a little higher. Yep, I was a mom, but I was still Shelley. I could still get dressed up and go out and about with the best of them!

Then, just as we were about to enter

the café inside Neiman Marcus, a woman stopped me and said ten words I'll never forget. "Did you know your baby spit up all over herself?"

With a feeling of doom, I looked into the stroller. And yep, there was little Lesley squirming and covered in baby goop. The moment she realized she had my attention, she did what babies do. She let out a piercing shriek. Loud enough to grab the attention of just about everyone in the middle of Neiman Marcus.

Minutes later, I was sitting in our red minivan changing Lesley's clothes and giving Arthur a couple animal crackers to tide him over. My husband saved the day by going through the drive-thru at McDonald's. Our trip to the mall was over.

Every time I think about that botched lunch at Neiman Marcus, I have to smile. It's the kind of thing that happens to everyone at one time or another, I think. Sometimes the best-laid plans just aren't meant to be!

Now I realize that that afternoon was simply life and that my desire to have lunch out was perfectly normal. I was thankful for my two tiny blessings, to have a good job, and to be a mom. All I needed was a little break! Perhaps that is what life is all about? Strollers and missed lunches and the ability to laugh at a situation that isn't perfect . . . but not wanting it any other way.

Years later, when my daughter was twelve or thirteen, we finally made it to Neiman Marcus. While we ate finger sandwiches and sipped tea, I told her all about her first trip there. She said she was glad I'd waited to return until she could actually enjoy the meal.

And of course, she was right. God's timing is everything.

Thanks for picking up the book. I hope you enjoyed *Thankful*. And, if you're a little bit like me, I hope you, too, take a moment to count your blessings. Even the not-so-perfect ones!

With blessings to you,
Shelley Shepard Gray ∿

Questions for Discussion

1. Much of *Thankful* revolves around one incident that changed both Christina's and Aden's lives. How might their lives have been different if Christina had never fallen through the ice? Do you think they would have stayed so close?

2. Is there an incident in your life that has acted as a turning point for you? What happened?

3. Another theme in *Thankful* is adoption, both literally and figuratively. Is there a person in your life whom you've "adopted"? Or have you become an honorary member of another family? How did that come about?

4. The moment I read the Amish proverb "If you can't have the best of everything, make the best of everything you have," I knew it fit Jana's story line. She had so many blessings, but she needed to give herself permission to do something new. When have you given yourself permission to "make the best of everything you have"?

5. Years ago my agent sent me a news article about Mennonite families fostering prisoners' children and it really struck a chord. I particularly have enjoyed writing about Judith and Ben's quest to have a family as well as their journey toward

becoming foster parents. What do you think will happen next with them? How do you think their experience with James will change them?

6. I loved the Scripture verse from Psalm 50: "Call on me when you are in trouble, and I will rescue you and you will give me glory." Has there been a time in your life when you called on God when you were in trouble? How do you think this verse relates to Christina and Judith?

7. Aden's grilled ham-and-cheese sandwiches come directly from my kitchen! I make grilled ham-and-cheese with Dijon mustard in a cast-iron skillet, and my kids always ask for them when they come home from college. Is there a comfort dish that is a particular favorite in your house? Who in your family makes it?

8. Which character in *Thankful* would you like to read more about in a future book? Why? ∾

Peanut Butter Pie

1 small box vanilla instant pudding
1¾ cups milk
4 ounces cream cheese, softened
⅓ of (8 ounce) tub of nondairy whipped
    topping
¼ cup peanut butter
⅔ cup powdered sugar
1 baked pie crust

Mix instant pudding with milk
according to directions on box. After
pudding sets, beat in softened cream
cheese and ⅓ tub of whipped topping.
In a separate bowl, blend peanut butter
and powdered sugar until crumbly.
When crust is cool spread ⅔ cup peanut
butter crumbles on bottom of crust. Fill
with pudding mixture and top with
remaining nondairy whipped topping.
Garnish with remaining peanut butter
crumbs. ❧

Taken from *Simply Delicious Amish
Cooking* by Sherry Gore. Copyright
© 2012 by Sherry Gore. Used
by permission of Zondervan.
www.Zondervan.com

A Sneak Peek of Shelley Shepard Gray's Next Book, *Joyful*

Light shines on the godly, and joy on those whose hearts are right.
                                        PSALM 97:11

A house is made from walls and beams . . . a home is made of love and dreams.
                                        AMISH PROVERB

RANDALL BEILER wasn't happy.

Perhaps that was putting things a bit harsh. Or maybe, rather, it was putting things a bit mildly.

Whatever it was, he needed something better in his life. A reason to be happy, a reason to be content. Or, as his little sister Kaylene was fond of saying, he needed something to be joyful about.

Unfortunately, he didn't think anything along those lines was going to happen anytime soon. Not while he had the combined weight of four of his younger siblings on his shoulders.

"Chicken again?" Levi griped as he entered the kitchen. "How many nights in a row have we had chicken? Something like eight?"

"I haven't been counting," Randall snapped. "If you know what's good for you, I wouldn't start counting, either."

"Is it grilled again?"

"Yep." Because he knew one way to cook chicken, and that was to grill it until it was almost charred.

Looking every bit of his fifteen years, Levi rolled his eyes. "Randall, can't you cook anything else?" ▶

"Nope." He knew how to bake potatoes, open jars of green beans that his sister Claire had put up, and grill chicken. That was the extent of his culinary skills.

Glaring at the plate of chicken, each portion looking a bit like a hockey puck, Levi didn't even try to hide his grimace of distaste. "Couldn't you at least try?"

With effort, Randall tried not to let his temper snap. "*Nee,* Levi, I cannot. As I've said before, if you want to take over the meals, go ahead. But as long as I'm cooking supper every night, we're going to have what I can cook."

"Which just happens to be grilled chicken, baked potatoes, and canned beans," Micah said as he wandered in with a grin. "At least dinner isn't full of surprises anymore. Claire loved her mystery-meat casseroles, she did."

Randall smiled, imagining the creations their bossy sister was preparing for her newlywed husband. "I'm sure Jim is pining for a piece of blackened chicken right about now."

"Doubt it," Levi grumbled.

Privately thinking that one of their eldest sister's casseroles would actually be a most welcome change, Randall picked up a plate and carried it to the table. "Where are Neil and Kaylene?"

"On their way. Kaylene wanted to help Neil with the goats," Micah said as he pointed toward the barn.

"Levi, go ahead and set the table then."

"Again? I set it last night."

"And I cooked last night. Do it."

With a sullen expression, his youngest brother set the table for five. By the time he'd gotten the last of the silverware in place, Kaylene and Neil had filtered in.

Micah filled up glasses with water, and then helped Randall fill the rest of the platters and carry them to the table. Then, after a brief prayer uttered gratefully in silence, they began to pass dishes and fill their plates.

Just as they'd done for all of Randall's twenty-one years.

In fact, the only thing that ever seemed to change was the number of placemats they set out . . . and who did the cooking.

Just five months ago, things had been a lot different. Their three older siblings, Junior, Beverly, and Claire had still been living at home. Those three had been managing things for years, ever since their mother had died soon after giving birth to Kaylene.

When their father died five years ago, they'd divided up even more duties. Beverly had taken over the house and sewing, Claire the cooking and finances. Junior had been in charge of them all, and had practically raised Kaylene by himself.

As fourth from the oldest, Randall had more or less skated under the radar. He'd gotten a job in construction as soon as he'd gotten out of school at fourteen, and had figured he was doing his part by contributing his paycheck to the family bank account.

Junior, being Junior, had let him believe he'd been doing enough.

Now Randall realized that he'd been only doing enough for himself. He'd worked and courted Elizabeth Nolt in his spare time. He'd always planned to ask Elizabeth to marry him when he'd been promoted to a supervisor. Whenever the time was right.

But then things had happened.

Junior had fallen in love with Miriam Zehr, Joe Burkholder had finally gotten up the nerve to ask their sister Beverly to marry him, and then Claire—to everyone's surprise—had up and married Jim Weaver and moved to Charm.

Three siblings married in less than three months!

Of course, all three of them had spent many an hour discussing the pros and cons of them leaving. Junior and Miriam had even volunteered to continue living at the farm to take care of them all.

But that had rubbed Randall the wrong way. He was a grown man, not a spoiled teenager. No way was he going to ever say that he couldn't handle what his older brother had been doing without complaint for most of his life.

Therefore, he and Micah and Neil had developed a new triumvirate. Micah did most of the farming and studied for his GED in his spare time. Neil continued to train dogs and breed his goats and pigs—all moneymakers.

And because he was now the eldest in the house, Randall had changed his life completely. He now only worked construction two days a week. The rest of the time he took care of the house, goaded Levi to do his chores and get to his part-time job, and ▶

tried his best to take care of the youngest member of their family, Kaylene.

Unfortunately, it seemed that he wasn't a very good mother. And his domestic skills were sadly lacking as well.

As the meal continued in silence, Randall tried to think of something to talk about. "Kay, did you see Miriam at school today?"

"*Jah.*"

"Why do you look so glum? I thought that would make you happy."

To his shock, Kaylene's eyes filled with tears. "Because she's . . . she's going to have a *boppli.*"

His fork clattered down on his plate. "What?"

Kaylene swiped her cheek with the side of her hand. "It's true."

"Well, that's a mighty big surprise," he murmured, feeling a little disappointed. Why hadn't Junior told him about the baby?

Levi turned to him in surprise. "Randall, you didn't know, either?"

"None of us knew," Micah said as he patted her cheek with his napkin. "Kay, how did you know?"

"Two of the kids were giggling about it. Saying Miriam looked like she was getting fat."

"I just saw her two weeks ago on Sunday," Randall said, trying to wrap his arms around the story. "We all did. She didn't look fat then."

"She doesna look fat, Randall," their little sister said impatiently. "She looks like she's gonna have a baby!"

Micah stared at Kaylene like she was sprouting whiskers. "Miriam and Junior have been married some time now," he said in his patient way. "I guess it's no surprise that a babe is on the way. Why are you crying?"

"Because now Junior is going to have his own family," she exclaimed, thick tears rolling down her cheeks. "He hardly comes over at all now. When he and Miriam have their own baby, I won't never see him no more."

"That would be won't *ever* see him," Micah murmured, absently correcting her grammar.

Kaylene scowled. "Oh, Micah, it don't matter, does it?"

"Well, um . . ." He looked to Randall for help.

Randall shrugged. They'd always depended on their smart brother to help with things like speech and grammar.

But that pause seemed to only make their sister even more perturbed.

Looking from Randall to Neil to Micah to Levi, the tears started falling even faster. "None of you are girls!" she cried, then left the table in a rush.

Stunned, Randall watched her run out of the kitchen. Silence reined around the table as the four of them listened to her scamper up the stairs, run down the hall, and then finally slam her door.

Alarmed, he looked at his brothers. "What was that about?"

"I could be wrong, but I'm thinking that she nailed it on the head," Micah said slowly. "We're not women and she needs one. Bad."

"Or Junior," Levi commented.

As much as he hated to admit it, he was starting to think that Kaylene had a very good point. "She needs a girl around, doesn't she?"

"She is nine now," Levi said. "I think girls that age need women around."

Randall was pretty sure Levi was right. "Do you think we should see if she could go live with Miriam and Junior? That might be best for her. You know she loves Miriam and she's always been closest to Junior."

Micah, being Micah, pondered that one for a long moment before shaking his head. "I don't think we should. That feels like we're pushing her on Junior, and that isn't right. They're newlyweds. Plus, if they've got a baby on the way, they've got other things to worry about."

"You've got a point, but we wouldn't be pushing Kay away. We would be trying to make her happy."

Levi frowned. "Somehow, I think that would make things worse. Besides, I don't think we're doing too bad."

"We?" Randall raised his brows.

"Come on. I'm around a lot more now. And I'm working. I don't think I'm doing anything worse than you did." ▶

"You're right." Randall sighed. Looking at his charred chicken and half-eaten baked potato, he wondered how such a bad supper had managed to get even worse.

"Randall, what about Elizabeth?" Neil asked.

"What about her?" He didn't even care that his bitter tone had directed everyone else at the table to look his way.

"You dated her for years. Can't you get her back?"

"And why would I want to do that?"

"If you married Elizabeth, she could live here." Warming to his idea, Neil added, "Then she could cook, clean, and help with Kay."

"First of all, Elizabeth broke up with me when I couldn't spend as much time with her as she wanted me to. Nothing's going to change anytime soon. And secondly, even if she did suddenly want to marry me, asking her to come here and cook and clean for the five of us ain't what most girls dream of doing when they get hitched."

Levi frowned. "You really don't like Elizabeth anymore? You courted her for two years."

No matter how much his pride stung, he couldn't say that he didn't like her. "All I'm saying is that some things are better in the past. Regrets are for fools, and I'm surely not that."

As his siblings slowly resumed eating, Randall felt the knot of disappointment resurface that had settled deep inside him when Elizabeth left.

No, he definitely didn't believe in regrets. But perhaps he was a fool after all, because he certainly did miss Elizabeth. He missed her something fierce.

Thank goodness no one else knew how much.

"You, Elizabeth, are a fool," Elizabeth Nolt mumbled to herself. "For sure and for certain."

Leaning back on her haunches, she squinted her eyes against the morning sun and surveyed the dinky row of carrots she'd just planted. If anything, they looked worse than the two rows of beans she'd planted yesterday.

One would think even a child could plant a decent vegetable garden. However, it seemed to be completely beyond her grasp.

"How are ya faring, Lizzy?" her grandmother called out from

where she sat on the porch swing. "It looks to me like you've been taking a bit of a breather."

"I needed one, I'm afraid." After slowly getting to her feet, Elizabeth dusted off her skirts. Then with a resigned sigh, she went to her grandmother's side. "I'm a poor gardener, Mommi, and that's a fact."

"I'm sorry to say this child, but it's true. Some days, I don't think you could get weeds to grow."

"I'm that bad?" She didn't even try to hide her amusement. Mommi Anna Mae was legally blind. She could hardly see the door in front of her, to say nothing of the not-so-beautiful garden. "And how can you be so sure?"

"Besides the fact that we've yet to eat anything you've tried to grow . . . I could hear you coughing and sighing and grunting from here on the porch. That's never a good sign."

"Mommi, I don't grunt."

"You don't sing when you're planting, either," she quipped.

When Elizabeth sat by her side, Anna Mae grabbed her hand. "You need to face it, dear. You are a poor gardener. We'll simply need to get our food from the grocery store like everyone else."

"Mommi, you know as well as I do that we need this garden to work. Food is expensive."

"Most everything is, it seems."

That was the Lord's honest truth. Over the last year things had become very tight in the Nolt household. Three years ago her mother had remarried and moved to Lancaster County in Pennsylvania. Though her mother had wanted Elizabeth to come along, Elizabeth hadn't been all that eager to live with a stepfather. Jim was a nice enough man, but he had particular ways of doing things, and Elizabeth knew she would have had to follow his rules.

Of course, that hadn't been the only reason she'd stayed behind. Though she'd volunteered to take care of her grandmother, everyone also knew that Elizabeth had only been biding her time until Randall Beiler had finally proposed.

And though, of course, she'd loved Randall for himself, it hadn't escaped her notice that the Beilers were one of the most prosperous families in Sugarcreek. When she married Randall, her financial troubles were going to be over. ▶

**A Sneak Peek of Shelley Shepard Gray's
Next Book, *Joyful* (continued)**

But unfortunately, he never did ask. He'd always been waiting for something, though what that was she never knew.

Then three of his siblings had gotten married, and one night he'd admitted that he was in no hurry to marry anytime soon, on account of his family needing him.

His confession hurt, almost as much as the way he'd hardly done more than quietly nod when Elizabeth had broken things off.

Almost as if their two years together had been nothing but a passing fancy.

To her shame, she realized that she'd been hoping that he would fight for her, even suggest that they marry and stay at his farm.

She would have done that gladly, too. She liked looking after other people. She liked cooking and sewing and planning and fussing.

But he never had run after her. Actually, he'd never even looked back.

Now she was trying to take care of her grandmother on a shoestring budget and spending the rest of her time living in the silence of her regrets.

She'd lost weight and couldn't seem to lift the cloak of disappointment that surrounded her now. It was a difficult thing to realize that one conversation could remove all the joy from her life.

It was even worse to realize that she had no earthly idea how to get it back. ∽